Twisted Starr 2
The Final Chapter

Twisted Starr 2
The Final Chapter

BY

TRACY WILSON

http://beautifulpublications.com

Published by
Beautiful Publications LLC
Stratford, CT 06614

This book is a work of fiction. Names, characters, places, and incidents are either products of the author's imagination or are used fictitiously. Any resemblance to actual events or locales or persons, living or dead, is entirely coincidental.

©Copyright 2019 Tracy Wilson

PRINT ISBN: 978-1-7331792-2-5
EBOOK ISBN: 978-1-7334002-2-0

Printed in the United States of America

Dedication

I dedicate this series to Starr.

Chapter 1

"Here she comes..." Beautiee said as Ms. Lemdon pulled up.

"She looks just like her picture..." Bazil said. They watched Ms. Lemdon get out of her car and come towards them.

"Hello Mr. Osgood – it's a pleasure to meet you..." she said as she shook his hand...

"It's nice to meet you too..." he said as he shook her hand. Bazil waited to see if she was going to acknowledge Beautiee...

"You must be Mrs. Osgood..." she said as she smiled...

"Call me Beautiee..."

"That's a lovely name – and it suits you..."

"Thank you!" Beautiee beamed as they walked towards the main entrance...

"You're welcome – and please call me Sheddi..." she said as she opened the door to let us inside. "As you can see, this is a corner unit with recent updates..."

"I see..." Bazil said as he walked around.

"The common charges include heat and hot water, and the roof was replaced 8 years ago."

"This is really cute…" Beautiee said…

"Does it have laundry?" Bazil asked…

"Yes – there's a coin-operated washer and dryer in the basement." Bazil bust out laughing. "Did I say something funny?" Sheddi asked…

"I can't believe they still use those…" Bazil laughed…

"Some places still do – so Beautiee – do you have any questions?"

"I like it – as long as my husband approves…"

"And do you approve Mr. Osgood?" Bazil didn't answer her – he just reached in his pocket and pulled out a certified cashier's check for $65,000. "Okay – I'll get this to the seller immediately – I have a copy of the contract if you'd like to sign it…"

"I'm sure there aren't any issues – please send it over to my attorney…"

"Of course – may I have his email?"

"J.Small@RC.com."

"What's his address – I'll put it in the contract…"

"280 Trumbull Street, Hartford, CT 06103 – 860-275-8238."

"Thank you Mr. Osgood – I'll get this right out – but I do have a question…"

"Yes Sheddi?"

"Why are you buying a one-bedroom? I have some rental properties you may be interested in that would generate a lot more income..."

"It's not for me – it's for my daughter..."

"Awww... that's nice – I'll get this right over to your attorney – we'll be in touch..."

"Okay – thank you Sheddi..."

"You're welcome – I'll see you soon..."

"Will you be at the closing?" Beautiee asked...

"Yes I will – if you like..."

"I'd like that..." Beautiee said as she smiled...

"Okay then – I'll see you in two weeks."

"Hey Chan..." I said as I answered the phone...

"Are you busy?"

"Mommy's here..."

"Listen – I need you to get your computer..."

"Okay – hold on..." I said as I put the phone down and I ran to get my computer..."

"Is that Chandler?" Mommy asked...

"Yes Mommy..." I breathed as I sat down and picked up the phone... "Okay – I got it..."

"Okay... I need you to type this in your browser...

"Okay..."

"www.jobapscloud.com/CT/#EmpDiv1"

"Okay… I'm there…"

"Scroll down to Secretary 1 in New Haven…"

"Okay… I'm there…"

"Good — apply for the position — the deadline is May 12th — once they have your application I'll make sure you get the job…"

"Why are you crying?" Mommy asked. I didn't answer here… I just looked at the page:

Secretary 1
Recruitment# 190501-6976CL-001
Location: New Haven, CT
Date Opened: 5/2/2019 12:00:00 PM
Salary: $42,684 - $56,009/year
Job Type: Open to the Public
Close Date: 5/12/2019 11:5900 PM
Southern Connecticut State University

I continued scrolling down the page as I read the Selection Plan, Purpose of Job Class, Duties, Knowledge, Skill and Ability, and Minimum qualification — General Experience…

"Chandler…"

"What's wrong?"

"Nothing… I love you so much…"

"I love you too…"

"I'm clicking on it now…"

"Okay…"

"Chandler?"

"Yes Starr?"

"They want my address…"

"Put my address…"

"Put your address?"

"Yes – this way you won't have to change your address after you're married…"

"Okay… I'll do it right now…"

"Okay – I'll put in a call on your behalf – the job is yours…"

"Okay Chandler… I'll see you tonight…"

"I can't wait…"

"Neither can I…"

"I love you…"

"I love you too…" Chandler said as he hung up…

"Starr… why are you crying?"

"Mommy… God answered my prayers…"

"He did?"

"Yes Mommy…"

"Yes Mary…" God said…

"Oh that's wonderful…" Mommy said as she pulled me into a hug…

"I prayed for a job… I prayed for my father… I prayed for you… and I prayed for Chandler…" I cried… "Thank you God…"

"Your welcome Starr…" God said…

"Hmmm… this is good… everything is going according to my plan…" Mommy thought to herself…

"No Mary – everything's going according to my plan…" God said.

Chapter 2

"Hey Smalls..." Bazil said as he answered the phone...

"Bazil... I got this contract... I have questions..."

"I knew you would..."

"What's going on Bazil?"

"I'm on my way..." Bazil said as he hung up the phone... "Beautiee... I need to go..."

"You need to give me some more dick too..." she said...

"I will... I promise..." he breathed as he pulled her into a kiss...

"Mmmm... you keep kissing me like that I'm locking you in here..."

"I'll be back later tonight..."

"Tonight?"

"Yes Beautiee..." Beautiee started to pout...

"I'll make it up to you... if you're up..."

"Oh I'll be up this time – the last time you left and came back late we found out you had a 22 year old..."

"And…" Bazil breathed as he kissed her neck… "We also found out…" Bazil breathed as he kissed her deeply… "We're going to have a baby…" he said and then he put his tongue in her mouth…

"Bazil…" Beautiee moaned…

"Yes… Beautiee…"

"Hurry back… please…"

"I will… I promise…" he breathed as he kissed her again, went downstairs, and left.

"Hey Valarie…" Bazil said as soon as he saw her…

"Hello Mr. Osgood – Smalls is expecting you – go right in…"

"Okay – thanks…" Bazil said as he went inside…

"Bazil!" Smalls exclaimed as he got up…

"Hey Smalls…" Bazil said as he embraced Smalls…

"It's been a minute…"

"Yes it has…"

"How's things with you and Beautiee?"

"She's pregnant…"

"Bazil – yo – why the fuck you ain't tell me man – congratulations!"

"Thank you…"

"Bazil – you're happy – right?"

"Yes…"

"Bazil… talk to me…"

"Sigh…"

"Sit down Bazil..." Bazil sat on the couch and Smalls sat beside him. "I see you're buying a one-bedroom co-op in Downtown Bridgeport..."

"Yes..."

"Why?"

"It's for my daughter..."

"Wait... oh shit!"

"Yea..."

"Bazil... tell me..."

"Starr is my daughter..."

"You're sure?"

"Yes..."

"Did you have a DNA test?"

"No..."

"How are you sure then?"

"Chandler compared my blood and DNA to Starr's Blood & Alcohol Assessment Test – it's a match..."

"Why does Chandler have Starr's Blood & Alcohol Assessment Test – no – fuck this – Bazil – what the fuck is going on?"

"Chandler sent me a text saying he needed to see me about my daughter – he said it was urgent – so I met with him..."

"Okay..."

"Before Mary got arrested she put Starr on her Section 8 Certificate so Starr wouldn't be out in the street..."

"Why would she be out in the street? What happened to Wayne?"

"He left Starr to fend for herself when she turned 18."

"Mutha fucka! Why?"

"Because he found out he wasn't Starr's father..." Bazil sighed...

"What does all this have to – never mind – go 'head."

"Starr was working but she lost her job. She's getting unemployment but it's about to run out. She's been keeping it together and staying focused but she's been struggling. She didn't reach out to me right away because she knew her mother would be upset. She had to go to DSS to recertify for Section 8 and that's where they did the Drug & Alcohol Assessment." Smalls sat there for a few moments processing what Bazil said... and then it hit him...

"Chandler's fucking your daughter..."

"Yes..."

"That's fucked up..."

"I took it that way too... at first... I knocked the shit outta Chandler..."

"I would've too..."

"I thought Chandler was playin' my daughter but he's not – he loves my daughter..."

"Chandler?"

"Yes..."

"Does Beautiee know?"

"She does now..."

"How'd she take it?"

"She went crazy..." Bazil whispered as he started crying...

"What happened?"

"Beautiee found out she was pregnant... she wanted to tell me... but before she could tell me she was pregnant I told her I have a daughter... and she needs my help..."

"So... you never told Beautiee about Starr?"

"No..."

"Bazil – she was in jail with your baby momma – and you didn't tell her?"

"I know – I know..." Bazil said as he stood up and pulled up his shirt...

"Oh shit – she did that?"

"Beautiee threw the table... threw the coffee pot, broke some glasses, and punched me in the jaw..."

"Got Damn!"

"She told me she wasn't sure she wanted my baby or this marriage... she took her rings off... and threw them at me..." Bazil cried...

"Damn Bazil... I'm sorry..."

"It broke my heart..."

"So... what about the baby?"

"She went to the doctor with Keisha... I went with Troy... we saw our baby... she forgave me..."

"You're a lucky man..."

"I'm a blessed man... God told me it was her choice... and she chose me... again..."

"Aww... I love y'all..." Smalls said as he started tearing up..."

"I love us too... I'm so happy..."

"Thank God..."

"You're welcome..." God said...

"Mary got paroled..."

"Where's she staying?"

"She's staying with Starr..."

"Bazil... Starr could lose her Section 8..."

"I know..."

"Wait a minute – is that why you bought this co-op? For Mary?"

"I bought it for Starr..."

"Bazil – you know Mary's staying there..."

"I know..."

"Bazil... are you sure this is a good idea?"

"No..."

"Bazil... you don't have to sign this contract..."

"Yes... I do..."

"Why?"

"Because Beautiee said I need to..."

"Beautiee? Your wife?"

"She found the place and suggested I buy it..."

"Damn Bazil – you must have some platinum dick!" Smalls laughed...

"I do... but that's not why she suggested it..."

"Why did she suggest it?"

"Beautiee says our daughter should have something in her name besides a Section 8 Certificate..."

"Damn..."

"Beautiee also says we need to get Starr out of public housing..."

"She has a point there..."

"Beautiee also said I'll be helping Starr invest in real estate..."

"You have a good wife..."

"I thank God for her every chance I get..."

"You know Mary will be there..."

"Beautiee says I should put my name on the title as well as Starr's so it can't be transferred without my signature..."

"She's right..."

"Beautiee also suggested we draw up a lease... for Mary..."

"Wait... what?"

"Beautiee said we should draw up a lease, sublet it to Mary, charge her rent, and let Starr pay the difference..."

"Beautiee really loves you..."

"Yes she does... and she love's Starr..."

"Okay... I feel better now... but I do have a question..."

"Okay..."

"Why are you buying her a co-op in Bridgeport?"

"So Starr can be close to her mother..."

"Starr won't be living there?"

"Starr's going to move in with Chandler…"

"And you're okay with that? You're okay with Chandler fucking your 22 year old daughter?"

"Chandler wants to marry my daughter…"

"He asked me for my blessing to ask for her hand – and I said yes… and he proposed…"

"Awww… Damn… I can't take it… I fuckin' love y'all…"

"He's a good man… my daughter's very happy…"

"That's what's up…"

"And Beautiee…"

"What about Beautiee?"

"We've been fucking non-stop…"

"My man!" Smalls said as he gave Bazil a pound…

"Starr caught us fuckin' the other day…"

"Oh shit…"

"I gave her a key… for emergencies…"

"Damn Bazil – you didn't tell her to call first?"

"No…" Bazil laughed…

"I bet that was awkward…"

"It was – she was embarrassed – and Beautiee was fuckin' pissed!" Bazil laughed…

"Oh shit – what happened?"

"Beautiee made us coffee, put her number in Starr's phone, then she told her you call your dad, you call me – if we don't answer, then you come over – and you call our name when you come in..." Bazil laughed...

"I don't think Starr will do that again...

"Naaa..."

"Okay Bazil – I'm good now – sign this contract so I can get it back to Ms. Lemdon..."

"Okay – where do I sign?"

"Here... and there..." Smalls said as he pointed to the places on the contract... "I guess I'll be making changes to your will soon...

"Yes you will... I need to provide for my children..." Bazil said as he got up to leave...

"Where you goin'?"

"I got pussy waitin' for me..."

"Yo – I can't – get the fuck outta here!" Smalls laughed...

"I love you man..."

"I love you too..." Smalls yelled down the hall as Bazil disappeared.

"Beautiee..." Bazil whispered...

"Bazil..." Beautiee yawned...

"I'm home..." he said as he climbed in bed with her...

"How'd everything go?" Bazil didn't answer her – he just pulled her naked body close to him and kissed her...

"Mmmm... that good huh?"

"That good..." Bazil said as he eased himself inside her...

"Ohhh... Bazil..." Bazil kissed her again, and then kissed her neck.... And then moved down to her breasts and began sucking them... "Ooohhh..." Beautiee moaned as he wrapped his arms up under her, held her tighter, and fucked her harder... "Bazil... Bazil... Bazil..."

"Mmmm... Shit..." Bazil moaned into Beautiee's neck...

"Bazil... Fuck..." Beautiee breathed as she spread her legs wider and Bazil thrust in deeper...

"Damn this pussy feels good..." Bazil breathed and then he kissed Beautiee fully...

"Hmmph... Hmmph... Hmmph..."

"Mmmph! Mmmph! Mmmph!"

"Hmmph... Hmmph... Hmmph..."

"Mmmph! Mmmph! Mmmph!"

"Hmmph... Hmmph... Hmmph..."

"Mmmph! Mmmph! Mmmph!" Bazil knew Beautiee was close to coming when she wrapped her legs behind his back and pulled him in deeper...

"Hmmph... Hmmph... Hmmph..."

"Mmmph! Mmmph! Mmmph!"

"Hmmph... Hmmph... Hmmph..."

"Mmmph! Mmmph! Mmmph!"

"Hmmph... Hmmph... Hmmph..."

"Mmmph! Mmmph! Mmmph!"

"Mmmmmmmmmmmmm..." Beautiee moaned in Bazil's mouth. Bazil continued thrusting slower and let Beautiee enjoy her orgasm's descent... and then he started fucking her hard again...

"Mmmph! Mmmph! Mmmph! Mmmph! Mmmmmmpppphhhh!" Bazil stayed inside Beautiee and continued kissing her until she fell asleep.

Chapter 3

"Hey Chan..." I sighed when I got inside and closed the door...

"How was your day?" Chandler asked as he pulled me into a kiss...

"Mmmm... fine..." I breathed...

"You start the job on Monday..."

"Chandler! Thank you! Thank you! Thank you!" I exclaimed as I jumped into Chandler's arms and he kissed me... and I started crying...

"Starr... don't cry..." Chandler whispered as he kissed my eyes and my lips...

"I can't help it... God gave me everything I prayed for..."

"God gave me everything I prayed for too..."

"Chandler... you prayed... for me?"

"I asked God to send me a wife..." he said as he kissed my neck... "And here you are..."

"Oh Chandler..."

"Come with me..." Chandler said as he took my hand and led me to the bedroom. Chandler held me close to him, kissed me, walked me back towards the bed, laid me down, and climbed on top of me...

"Oh Chandler..." I moaned as Chandler put my hands up over my head and kissed me. Chandler got between my legs on his knees and took his time undressing himself as I watched. When he got to his waist I reached out to help him but Chandler stopped me...

"Put your hands back where they were... and be still..."

"Okay..." I breathed. Chandler took his time sliding his pants down off his waist, keeping eye contact with me to make sure I was watching. After he slid his pants down his thighs, he started getting erect and I liked what I saw. Chandler came close to me and began unbuttoning my blouse. My chest was heaving up and down in anticipation of what was coming next. Chandler laid on top of me, put his hands underneath me, unclasped my bra, pulled my breasts out from under the bra, and started sucking them as he was squeezing them... "Chandler..." I moaned as I arched my back and Chandler continued sucking and squeezing my breasts for a few moments. Chandler moved his hands down to my waist, unbuttoned my jeans, and took his time unzipping my zipper. I moved my hands again and Chandler stopped me...

"Ah ahh ahh... put your hands back where I had them..."

"Okay..." I breathed. Chandler began sliding my jeans off my waist, making sure my panties slid off along with them, until they were down at my ankles. Chandler took my shoes off my feet, slid my jeans and panties off, came up my body, spread my legs, eased himself inside me, and began thrusting... "Oh Chandler!" I moaned. I tried to hold him but he stopped me...

"What... did... I... tell... you... about... these... hands?" he asked between thrusts...

"Chandler... I..." Chandler moved my hands above my head and held them there so I couldn't move them while simultaneously kissing me...

"Ch..." was all I could moan before Chandler put his tongue in my mouth...

"Hhhhh... Hhhhh... Hhhhh... Hhhhh..."

"Mmmph! Mmmph! Mmmph! Mmmph!" Chandler had me pinned down beneath his body... and his mouth... he was in complete control... all I could do was submit... and enjoy...

"Hhhhh... Hhhhh... Hhhhh... Hhhhh..."

"Mmmph! Mmmph! Mmmph! Mmmph!" I threw my legs up and locked them behind his back, pulling him in deeper...

"Hhhhh... Hhhhh... Hhhhh... Hhhhh..."

"Mmmph! Mmmph! Mmmph! Mmmph!"

"Hhhhhhhhh!" I moaned into Chandler's mouth as I arched my back and came. Chandler didn't stop... he kept going hard... and it felt so good...

"Mmmmmmppphhh!" Chandler stayed inside me as I relaxed my legs and continued kissing me. When he finally let go of my hands and tried to get up, I pulled him back down and kissed him hard... "Damn..." Chandler breathed. I didn't say anything... I just held him and kissed him... "We need to talk..."

"No..."

"Starr..." he said between kisses... "We... need... to... talk.."

"Okay..."

"I want to get married right away..."

"Okay..."

"Starr..."

"Yes Chandler?"

"Are you listening to me?"

"You... want... to... get... married... right... away..."

"Starr..."

"Yes... Chandler..."

"I... can't... have... a... conversation... like... this..."

"So... stop... talking... then..." Chandler took my hands, placed my hands above my head, put his tongue in my mouth, and started making love to me again.

Chapter 4

"Happy... Mother's... Day..." Bazil said between kissed as he kissed Beautiee's belly...

"Mmmm..." Beautiee moaned as she stretched and tried to sit up...

"Lay back down..." Bazil said as he pushed her back down...

"Okay..." Beautiee breathed as Bazil held her belly on both sides and kissed her belly all over...

"I love you..." Bazil whispered to Beautiee's belly as he continued kissing it and started to massage it...

"Oh Bazil... your hands..." Beautiee moaned...

"and I love..." Bazil said as he kissed his way down to Beautiee's pelvis... "That you're coming from here..." he said as he licked Beautiee's clit...

"Ohhh..." Beautiee moaned...

"Now..." Bazil said as he kissed Beautiee's inner left thigh... "I know you can't wait..." Bazil said as he kissed Beautiee's inner right thigh... "to meet me..."

"Ooohhh..." Beautiee moaned...

"but right now..." Bazil said as he licked Beautiee's clit again...

"Ooohhh... Beautiee moaned...

"your mother needs me..." Bazil said as he kissed her pussy lips... "to make her feel good..."

"Oh Bazil..." Beautiee moaned...

"so..." Bazil said as he kissed her pussy lips again... "I'll talk to you later..." and then he spread Beautiee's legs... and dove in...

"Baaazzziiilll!" Beautiee moaned as Bazil got down between Beautiee's legs, grabbed her ass in his hands, and sucked and licked hungrily...

"Ooohhh! Oooohhh! OOoohhhh!" Beautiee was soaking wet and Bazil stuck his tongue in her pussy and sucked her juices... "Ooohhhh! Bazil!" Beautiee moaned as he continued devouring her... "Bazil! Bazil! Fuck! I'm cumming!" she screamed as she grabbed the blanket in her hand and arched her back. Bazil lifted Beautiee's legs up on his shoulders, lifted her ass up off the bed, and shook his head back and forth between her legs, pushing his nose under, then over the hood of her clit as he came up under her clit with his tongue... "Aaahhh... Aaahhh.... Aaaahhhh!" Beautiee screamed as her legs shook around Bazil's head. Bazil continued to enjoy his liquid breakfast as Beautiee's orgasm subsided. Beautiee relaxed her legs on Bazil's shoulders and Bazil came up between her legs, got on his knees, and bent down to kiss her...

"Mmmm...." Beautiee moaned as Bazil put his tongue in her mouth and she started sucking it...

"Taste's... good... doesn't... it?" Bazil breathed...

"Yes..." Beautiee moaned. Bazil got up on his knees, lifted Beautiee up by her waist, and eased himself inside her... "Ohh... Bazil..." Beautiee moaned as she rode his dick while he held her up...

"Beautiee... shit..." Bazil moaned as he held on tighter and started thrusting inside her a little harder...

"Bazil..."

"Beautiee..."

"Bazil... Fuck me..." Bazil started pounding her pussy as she continued moaning... "Ooohhh... Ooohhh..."

"Uuugh! Uuugh! Uuugh!"

"Ooohhh! Oooohhh! Oooohhh!"

"Uuugh! Uuugh! Uuugh!"

"Baaazzziiill!"

"Uuuugggh! Uuuuuuggghhh!" Bazil continued thrusting slower as Beautiee's orgasm subsided... "Damn... I... could... stay... in... your... pussy... all... day..." Bazil breathed as he lowered Beautiee back down onto the bed, propped himself up on his hands, and continued thrusting...

"Feels... good... to... me..." Beautiee breathed...

"I'm... going... to... feed... you... both... and... then... I'll... be... right... back... inside... you..."

"Ooohhh... okay... hurry..."

"Mmmmppphhh... shit... I... will..."

"Good morning..."Chandler said as he kissed me awake...

"Mmmm... good morning..." I said as I pulled Chandler into another kiss...

"Uh Uh..." Chandler said as he got up outta bed...

"We're going to talk..." Chandler said as he left the bedroom and went into the kitchen. I got up out the bed, followed Chandler into the kitchen, wrapped my arms around him, and began kissing him on his neck... "Starr..." Chandler said as he turned around, pulled me close to him, and kissed me fully...

"Yes Chandler..."

"I... want... you..."

"I... want... you... too..."

"Starr... stop..."

"Why?"

"Go put some clothes on – then come sit here with me – we need to talk..."

"Okay..." I sighed.   I went into the bedroom, put on Chandler's shirt, and came back into the kitchen...

"You're not dressed..."   I walked over to Chandler and wrapped my arms around his neck...

"Are you upset with me?"

"No... sit down..."

"Okay..."

"Starr..."

"Yes Chandler?"

"I want us to get married... as soon as possible..."

"Okay..."

"Are you sure?"

"Well..."

"Talk to me..."

"It's just..."

"Starr..." Chandler whispered as I started to cry. Chandler got up, come over to me, and held me as I cried. "Starr..." Chandler said as he lifted my face by my chin and kissed me... "Don't cry... please..."

"I want my mother..."

"I don't understand..."

"At my wedding..."

"Who said she can't be there?"

"My father..."

"Bazil told you your mother can't be at your wedding?"

"No..."

"I don't understand…"

"I want my mother… and my father… at my wedding…"

"You mother will be there…"

"What about my father?"

"Starr…"

"Yes?"

"This is our wedding day…"

"Yes… but…"

"Starr… listen…"

"Okay…"

"Your mother… and your father… will be at our wedding… I promise…"

"Really? You promise?"

"I promise…"

"I love you Chandler…"

"I love you too… now…" he said as he kissed me… "We goin' talk… about… our… wedding… okay?"

"Yes Chandler…"

"Okay… we need to go down to City Hall and apply for our marriage license…"

"You need a license to get married?"

"Yes… you do…"

"Wow…"

"After we get our marriage license, we can get married in 48 hours…"

"Can it be later?"

"How much later?"

"I want to get a beautiful wedding dress, I want to get my hair done, I want to get a pedicure, a manicure... and I want to get something special... for our wedding night..."

"Okay..."

"And I want to get married in a church..."

"No problem..."

"And I want a romantic honeymoon..."

"Okay..."

"And..." I said as I stood up, walked over to him, opened his pants, took his dick out, and climbed on his lap... "I want to practice... for our wedding night..." I said as I sat on his dick and started riding...

"Starr... Ooohhh.... Shit..." Chandler moaned as he held me tighter. I moved down on his dick until it was up inside me completely and let out a moan...

"Chandler..." Chandler grabbed me by my ass and pushed me down on his dick, meeting my thrusts as he breathed in my neck...

"Uugh! Uugh! Uugh!"

"Chandler... Chandler... Chandler... Ooohhh!"

Uugh! Uugh! Uugh! Uugh!" Chandler breathed as we rocked the chair back and forth...

"Chandler... wait..." I breathed...

"You okay?" Chandler asked as he stopped and looked up at me...

"Come with me..." I breathed as I got up and headed into the bedroom. When I got there I jumped up on the bed, laid down, and put my arms up over my head. Chandler got up on the bed, thrust himself inside me, pinned my hands above my head, and began thrusting...

"Is this whatchu want?"

"Yes... Chandler... yes..." Chandler kissed me hard and put his tongue in my mouth as I started coming... "Huhh... Huhh... Huhh..."

"Mmmph! Mmmph! Mmmph!"

"Huhh... Huhh... Huhh..."

"Mmmph! Mmmph! Mmmph!"

"Hhhhuuuuhhhh! Hhhhuuuuhhh!" I moaned in Chandler's mouth as my legs trembled...

"Mmmmmpphh! Mmmmmpphh! Starr..."

"Yes... Chandler..."

"I... want... you... to... take... a shower..."

"Okay..."

"And get dressed..."

"Okay..."

"I have... a surprise... for you..."

"Chandler..."

"Yes... Starr..."

"I... can't... take a... shower..."

"Why..."

"Because... you won't... stop... kissing... me..."

"Okay... I'll... stop..." Chandler said and then he got up...

"Where are you going?"

"Hurry up and get dressed – I'll be right back..." Chandler said as he hurried out and I heard the door close.

Chapter 5

"Who is it?" Mary asked as she went to the door and peeked out the peep hole.... "Oh shit – damn – I'm not supposed to be here – shit, shit, shit!"

"Mary?"

"Are you here to arrest me?"

"Hell no!" Chandler laughed...

"Then why are you here?"

"I'm here for Starr..."

"She's not here..."

"I know..."

"Oh my God – is everything okay?"

"Mary – please open the door..."

"You promise I'm not under arrest?"

"I promise..."

"Okay..." Mary said as she opened the door and let Chandler inside. "Is Starr in trouble?"

"Mary..." Chandler said as he took Mary's hand and kissed it... "I'm Chandler..."

"You're Chandler? Sergeant Chandler?"

"Yes..."

"Oh wow – it's nice to meet you... finally..."

"I thought you knew who I was?"

"I knew who you were – but I've never met you – I heard about you from Thompson..."

"Oh – listen – I need you to do me a favor..."

"Okay..."

"I need you to take this phone..."

"Why are you giving me a phone?"

"I'll explain in the car..."

"Oh hell no – I'm not going anywhere with you – get out!"

"Mary – please – trust me..."

"Why?"

"Because I love your daughter..."

"Well... alright... I'll go..."

"Good – c'mon!" Chandler said as he ran out the apartment and down the stairs...

"What the hell is he up to?' Mary asked out loud as she closed the door, locked it, and went downstairs. When she saw the squad car she hesitated...

"Get in Mary..." Chandler said as he rolled down the window...

"In the front?"

"Yes Mary..."

"I don't know what's going on... but – fuck it..." she said as she got in the car and sat down...

"Put your seat belt on..." Chandler said as he started the car...

"Where are we going?"

"You'll see…" Chandler answered as he pulled off and started driving down the street. Mary sat there quiet, observing Chandler as he drove. She was relieved when she saw Chandler smiling until they got near Downtown Bridgeport. She sat quiet and didn't say anything as they drove past the court house. When they got closer, Chandler slowed down and entered the parking lot. Chandler pulled up in front of the main entrance and parked the car. "We're here…"

"Where are we?" Mary asked…

"We're at my place…"

"Your place?"

"Mary…" he said as he reached over and unbuckled her seat belt… "Trust me…"

"Okay…" she sighed as she went to open the door…

"Uh uh!"

"What's wrong?"

"Let me get the door for you…" Chandler said as he got out the car, went around to the other side, and opened the door for Mary…

"Thank you…"

"You're welcome…"

"Good afternoon Mr. Chandler…" the doorman said as he held the door open.

"Good afternoon…" Chandler said as he walked inside and Mary followed him to the elevator…

"This is a really nice building..." Mary said as she looked around...

"Thank you... it is..." Chandler said as the elevator doors opened. Mary went inside, Chandler followed, and pushed the floor. When the elevator stopped and the doors opened, Chandler spoke... "I'm going to go inside first to make sure Starr is ready – after I go inside, I want you to call her with that phone – tell her you're on your way to see her, and then come inside..."

"Okay..." Mary said as she stood outside in the hallway...

"Starr..."

"Yes Chan – I'm in the kitchen – I made a pot of coffee..." I said as Chandler came into the kitchen...

"Starr – is that your phone ringing?"

"Oh shoot – I'll be right back..." I said as I ran to get my phone... "Mommy!"

"Hey baby girl!"

"Happy Mother's Day Mommy!"

"Thank you baby..."

"I miss you Mommy..."

"I miss you too..."

"I wish I could see you..."

"I'm on my way..." my mother said as she hung up and came inside. Chandler motioned for her to come into the kitchen and I started to cry... "Mommy!"

"Oh Starr... my baby... come here..." my mother said as she pulled me into a hug and held me...

"This was your surprise?" I asked as I looked at Chandler...

"Yes..."

"I love you so much!" I squealed as I ran to him and started kissing him all over his face...

"I love you too..." Chandler laughed... "Now... let's have some coffee..." Chandler said as Mary sat down at the table. I took down three cups, poured the coffee, added the hazelnut creamer, added the sugar, and placed them on the table...

"Mommy – did you know about this?"

"Hell no – I thought I was under arrest!" my mother laughed...

"For what Mommy?"

"I'm not supposed to be in your apartment – I thought somebody ratted me out!" my mother laughed...

"We don't arrest people for Section 8 violations – unless they're slinging or we find guns..." Chandler said...

"I'm so happy you're here Mommy..."

"I'm happy to baby..."

"So..." Chandler interrupted... "Before I came to pick you up, we were talking about the wedding...

"Oh – I can't wait..." my mother said...

"You won't have to wait long..." Chandler said...

"I just wish I could be there..."

"You will be..." Chandler said...

"I will?" my mother asked...

"Of course..."

"What about Bazil?"

"He's not my Mother-In-ln-Law — you are..." Chandler said as he took my mother's hand and kissed it...

"My daughter's a lucky woman..."

"I'm the lucky one..." Chandler said as he got up and kissed my mother on the cheek...

"Aww... you're very sweet..."

"Mary... listen here..." he said as he took my mother's hand...

"Yes Chandler?"

"You're very important to Starr... that means you're very important to me..."

"Thank you Chandler..."

"Whatever's going on between you and Bazil — that's between you and Bazil..."

"You're right..."

"The most important thing is Starr's happiness..."

"I couldn't agree more..."

"He game me his blessing... you gave me your blessing... she said yes... and that's all that matters..."

"Yes it is..." I sat there and watched Chandler finish his coffee as my mother finished hers. "Now..." Chandler said as he got up... "We need to go... we have reservations... at Testos..."

"Oh my God! I've always wanted to go to Testos!" my mother squealed.

"I've never been to Testos..." I said...

"Ladies... you're in for a special treat... Chandler said as we followed him out the door. When we got downstairs we went to the car and waited for Chandler to open the door for us, then we both got in. Chandler got in, started the car, and pulled off.

"This is the best Mother's Day I've had in a long time..." my mother said.

"It's not over yet..." Chandler said as we pulled into the parking lot. Chandler parked the car, opened the door for us, and we both got out.

"Oh my God – it's so beautiful out here..." my mother said.

"Wait till you see inside..." Chandler said as he held the door open for us...

"Oh wow!" my mother and I said in unison...

"Is this your first time here?" the hostess asked.

"Yes..." we both answered in unison as we laughed...

"Mr. Chandler – your table's ready – right this way..." the manager said as he came out to escort us to our table.

"Oh wow... it's beautiful – look Mommy – a fire place!"

"Oh Chandler – this is lovely – thank you so much..." my mother said...

"You're welcome Mary..." Chandler said as we waited for Chandler to pull out our chairs and then we sat down.

"Shall I get the menu?" the server asked as he put bread and butter on the table...

"Yes – thank you..." Chandler said. We each had some bread with butter while we waited for the menu.

"Shall we start with something to drink?" the server asked as we looked at the menu...

"I'll have a whiskey sour..." Chandler said...

"I'll have an amaretto sour..." my mother said...

"Ooohhh... that sounds good..." I said...

"She'll have one too..." my mother said...

"I'll be back with your drinks..." the server said...

"Everything looks so good... I can't decide between the broiled scallops and the open steak..." my mother said...

"Get 'em both..." Chandler said...

"Chandler... I can't... that's too much food..."

"Starr will help you – and if she doesn't – take it home..."

"Really? You're sure?"

"Of course..."

"Okay then!"

"I'ma get the open steak... with fries..."

"Hot damn – a man that knows what he wants!" my mother said...

"Damn right I do..." he said as he pulled me into a kiss...

"Are you ready to order?" the server asked...

"I'm read – I'll have the broiled scallops and the open steak..." my mother said...

"The broiled scallops come with linguini in a white claim sauce – is that alright?"

"Oh yes..." my mother said...

"And what would you like?" he asked me...

"I'd like the cheese ravioli..."

"That's all you're gonna eat?" my mother asked...

"I'm gonna help you eat the broiled scallops and linguini with white claim sauce too..." I laughed...

"And you sir?" the server asked Chandler...

"I'ma have the open steak..."

"Coming right up..." the server said as he took the menu and went to place our order. We drank, laughed, talked, and finished the bread while we waited for our food. When the server brought our food to the table my eyes got really big...

"Oh my God! There's so much food!" I exclaimed...

"We can handle it..." my mother laughed...

"I know I can — and I'm about to..." Chandler said as he picked up his fork...

"Chandler... wait..." my mother said...

"Okay..."

"Starr... take my hand..." my mother said as I took her hand and she took Chandler's hand. "Take Chandler's hand..." my mother said. I took Chandler's hand and then my mother prayed... "Heavenly father... we thank you for this food, for your blessings... for my daughter... and for my son-in-law... amen."

"Amen!" Chandler and I said in unison...

"You're welcome..." God said.

"Can I go in now?" Chandler asked...

"Sure can!" my mother said as we started eating...

"Oh my God! This food is so good! It's been so long!" my mother said...

"It is good..." I said. Chandler didn't say anything — he just ate his food.

"You 'bout ready to help your mother with these scallops & linguini?" my mother asked...

"Sure am!" I said as I helped myself to half the plate...

"Damn girl — you hungry?" my mother laughed...

"I can't help it..." I laughed... "This is sooo good..."

"It is good... especially these scallops..." my mother said as she picked another scallop up with her fork. Chandler smile as he watched us eat. "You ready Chandler?" my mother asked...

"I'm good – I ate – enjoy your food..." Chandler laughed...

"I'm full..." I laughed as I dropped my fork on my plate..."

"Haa Haa! I knew you couldn't hang with your mama!" my mother laughed as she took my plate and finished it...

"Would you like any dessert?" the server asked when he came over...

"Oh no... I'm done!" I laughed...

"And you sir?" he asked Chandler...

"I'm good – you want dessert Mary?"

"No thank you – I'm good..." my mother laughed...

"Very well... I'll be back with your check..." the server said as she walked away...

"Oooohhhh!" Chandler yelled as he stretched and then got up...

"Here's your check Mr. Chandler..." the server said as he put it on the table. Chandler signed the check, I got up with my mother, and we all went out to the car. Chandler opened the door for us, we got in, Chandler closed the doors, and then took out his cell phone...

"Who's he calling?" my mother asked...

"Who knows?" I lied. I knew Chandler was calling my father...

"Yes Chandler?" Bazil said as he answered the phone...

"We're on our way..." Chandler said and then he hung up...

"Chandler's on his way..." Bazil said to Beautiee...

"Thank God he called first..." Beautiee said as she got up outta bed...

"You're welcome..." God laughed...

"Mary – I'ma drop you off and then I'm taking Starr..." Chandler said as he got in the car...

"Okay – thank you again Chandler...

"You're welcome..." Chandler said as he started the car and pulled off. We didn't talk on our way to drop my mother off. When we got to the apartment I started to get sad and Chandler saw it... "Starr..." Chandler said as he touched my hand... "You'll see your mother again – I promise..." Chandler parked the car, got out, opened the door for my mother... and I jumped out the car before he could open the door for me... "Mommy..." I whispered as I grabbed her and hugged her tight...

"I love you too... I'll see you soon..." I let her go, got back in the car, and started to cry as my mother went into the building. Chandler didn't say anything – he just let me cry as we drove to Milford to see my father.

"Hey Chandler – c'mon in.." Bazil said as he opened the door... "Hey Starr..."

"Hi Daddy..." I said as I walked past him... and he pulled me back into his arms...

"What's wrong Starr?" he asked as he held me...

"I miss my mom..."

"You're going to be spending more time with your mother real soon..." he said as he kissed me on my forehead..."

"I know... I just miss her..."

"Hey Starr!" Beautiee beamed as she came down the stairs towards me...

"Oh my God! Beautiee... you're glowing!"

"Awww... thank you!" Beautiee said as she hugged me... "Bazil... look!" Beautiee exclaimed as we all looked at her stomach...

"Oh my goodness..." I laughed... "I guess my little brother is happy to see me too..." I said as I touched her stomach...

"A boy?" Beautiee asked...

"A boy..." my father and I both said in unison...

"Congratulations Bazil..." Chandler said. My father didn't say anything – he just came over to us, pulled me into a hug along with Beautiee, and cried...

"Daddy... stop crying..."

"I can't help it... I have a beautiful wife... a beautiful daughter... and I'm having a beautiful son..."

"Ummm... what about me?" Chandler laughed...

"And... I'm getting a beautiful son-in-law..." Bazil laughed...

"What – no tears for me?" Chandler laughed...

"C'mon – let's go sit down..." Beautiee said as we all went to sit in the living room...

"Happy Mother's Day Beautiee..." I said...

"Thank you Starr..."

"I'ma make this quick..." Chandler interrupted...

"What's going on Chandler?" my father asked...

"Starr starts work tomorrow..."

"Starr! Congratulations!"

"Thank you Daddy..."

"When did this happen?" Beautiee asked...

"Chandler found the job for me... he told me all I had to do was fill out the application and the job was mine..."

"That's great! Where will you be working?"

"I'll be working at the State Connecticut University in New Haven..."

"Thank you Chandler..." my father said...

"You're welcome..."

"Does your mother know?" Beautiee asked...

"Yea... she knows..." I answered...

"We need to talk about the wedding..." Chandler interrupted...

"Okay…" my father said…

"We're getting married right away…"

"Okay…"

"Starr wants a church wedding…"

"No problem…"

"And Starr wants her mother at her wedding…"

"Okay…"

"Really Daddy?"

"Of course…" my father said as he kissed me on my forehead and pulled me next to him…

"Thank you Daddy…"

"You don't have to thank me…"

"See Starr… I told you…" Chandler said…

"Yes Chandler… you did…"

"We have a surprise for you – we were going to wait but we might as well tell you now…

"What Daddy – what?"

"I bought you a co-op in Downtown Bridgeport…"

"Oh Daddy – thank you, thank you, thank you! When do I get the keys?"

"We close in another week – I'll let you know – you need to be there to sign documents…

"Mommy's going to be so happy…"

"Starr…"

"Yes Daddy…"

"You mother has to sign a rental agreement…"

"I'm not charging my mother rent Daddy…"

"Starr..."

"I won't do it Daddy..."

"Starr..."

"Daddy... please..."

"Starr..."

"Yes Daddy..." I sighed...

"The title will be in your name... and mine..."

"Okay..."

"I know you'll let your mother stay in the co-op... and she can stay... as long as she signs the rental agreement..."

"How much rent does she have to pay?"

"The co-op has an HOA fee – your mother's rent goes towards that fee – we can work that out later... but whatever it is... you have to pay the difference..."

"Hmmm... okay..."

"The best thing is you'll be out of public housing... you won't need your Section 8 anymore... and you can see your mother as often as you want..." I didn't say anything – I just looked at Chandler.

"Come here Starr..." Beautiee said as she got up. She started walking towards the library and I followed her inside and sat down. "I know you're disappointed..." she said as she took my hand... "but this will be good for both of you...

"How? How is charging my mother rent good for me? She couldn't afford the rent we had

– that's why she had Section 8 in the first place..." I said as I started crying...

"Come over here with me Starr..." I sat down at the desk and she turned on the computer. I watched her log on to realtor.com and put the address in. I started to feel better when I saw the picture...

"That's a corner unit?"

"Yes Starr..."

"Hmmm... It's kinda cute – it'll be good for my mom – she won't have to walk up a lot of stairs..."

"Exactly..."

"Oh... this is nice..." I said when I saw the living room...

"We thought so too..."

"The kitchen is small... but it's cute – it lets in a lot of light – my mom will like that..."

"I like that too – you won't have to have lights on all the time..."

"I like the bathroom..."

"I like that too..."

"Daddy says it has an association fee – that's that?"

"The association mows the lawn, takes the garbage, and shovels the snow... stuff like that..."

"Oohhh... Mommy will really like that..."

"It's good for you too – you don't need to be outside doing that stuff..."

"So... how much is everything?"

"Click on the payment calculator and it will show you..." I clicked on the payment calculator and saw the following:

Principal & Interest	$256
Property Tax	$139
Home Insurance	$ 21
HOA Fees	$304
	$720 Month

Home Price $65,000
Down Payment $13,000 – 20%

"I'm not sure I can afford this – I just started working – and my mom doesn't have any money..."

"Starr..."

"Yes Beautiee?"

"Your father bought this for you..."

"I know he put the down payment – but $720 is a lot of money..."

"Starr..."

"Yes Beautiee?"

"Your father bought this for you..."

"You mean... Daddy bought this... for $65,000 – for me?"

"Yes Starr..."

"Oh Wow..."

"Now do you think you can afford it?"

"I think so – do I have to pay for heat and hot water?"

"No – that's included in your common charges..."

"What's common charges?"

"The HOA Fee..."

"Oh okay – so I pay $304, plus $21, plus $139... let's see – that $464 a month – oh yea – I can afford that..."

"We thought so too..."

"Do I have to pay for electricity?"

"Yes..."

"Is that expensive?"

"It won't be as much as we pay for this house..." Beautiee laughed...

"Do I have to go to the laundry mat?"

"No – there's coin-operated machines in the basement..."

"Where is this?"

"It's Downtown Bridgeport – just a short walk away from Chandler..."

"Oh... that's nice..."

"Put in chandler's address in google..."

"Okay..." I said as I took the computer and did what she said...

"Now put going to your new address..." I did what she said and the map came up showing me the route...

"Oh wow... this is right down the street from Chandler..."

"Click on the first bus..."

"Okay..."

"See — your mom can take the #4 from Park Avenue and Jackson Avenue..."

"I see..."

"Now click on the 2nd bus..."

"Okay..."

"See — your mom can take the #3 from Madison Avenue and Thorme Street...

"Now click on the car..."

"Oh wow — it's only 9 minutes away by car..."

"See?"

"Thank you Beautiee..." I said as I hugged her...

"You're welcome Starr — but I'm not the one you need to thank..."

"Yes you are — you're the one that talked to my dad — I love you..."

"I love you too Starr..."

"Everything okay in here?" Chandler said as he came in...

"Everything's fine Chandler..." I said...

"Good — 'cause I need to spend some quality time with you before you go to work tomorrow..."

"Okay Chandler..." I said as it got up and we went into the foyer...

"You still mad at me?" my father asked...

"No Daddy — I said as I hugged him...

"Good..." he said as he kissed my forehead...

"I love you..."

"I love you too Daddy…"

"Good night Starr…" Beautiee said as she hugged me…

"Good night Beautiee – good night lil' brother…" I said as I kissed her stomach and he moved…

"Good night son…" Beautiee laughed as she pulled Chandler into a hug…

"Yes… good night son…" my father laughed as he hugged Chandler…

"Oh boy – I guess I have this to look forward to…" Chandler laughed…

"You sure do…" my father laughed as he opened the door… "Starr – I'll let you know when to come sign the documents and get your keys…"

"Okay Daddy – good night…" When we got to the car Chandler pulled me into a kiss and held me… "Mmmm…. What was that for?" Chandler didn't answer me – he just opened the door, helped me in, closed the door, then got in himself… "I had a great day Chandler…"

"So did I… and I'm looking forward to a great night…" Chandler said as he smiled mischievously, started the car, and drove us home. When we got upstairs I couldn't wait to call my mother and tell her the good news…

"Hey Starr… how was your day?"

"Mommy – you're not going to believe this…"

"Believe what honey?" Chandler snatched the phone out my hand before I could answer…

"Starr's busy now... she'll talk to you tomorrow..." Chandler said and then he hung up my phone, took me by the hand, and led me into the bedroom.

Chapter 6

"Hi Mommy..." I answered...

"Where are you?"

"I'm on the train..."

"Oh – that's right – you started work today – how was it?"

"It's college Mommy – busy, busy, busy!" I laughed...

"Think you can handle it?"

"Mommy – it's the same as working for City Hall – they just want everything yesterday..."

"So you're staying?"

"They asked me the same thing..." I laughed...

"Really?"

"Yea – they had a few people quit on them already..."

"That busy huh?"

"It is – but I like being busy..."

"They must be happy to have you..."

"Oh they're definitely happy – the last person they hired left for lunch and never came back…" I laughed…

"Wow…"

"Mommy… I have something to tell you…"

"Oh – that's right – Chandler took the phone before you could tell me – what's going on?"

"I'll tell you when I get there…"

"You're coming here?"

"Yes Mommy – I need to see you…"

"I'm always happy to see you – but this sounds serious…"

"It is… I'll see you soon Mommy…"

"Okay Starr…" she said as she hung up. I was afraid to tell my mother. I knew she'd be happy but how is she going to react when she finds out my father is charging her rent? As I got closer to Bridgeport I began dreading the conversation…

"Hey Chan…" I answered…

"What's wrong?"

"Nothing…"

"Bad day?"

"Chan – I had a great day…"

"Oh so you like the job?"

"I love it…"

"Whew – you had me worried…"

"I was telling my mother they're happy to have me – the last person they had left for lunch and never came back…" I laughed…

"Damn!"

"It doesn't bother me – I'm used to it – I used to work in City Hall..." I laughed...

"So what are your hours?"

"Monday through Thursday – 8:30 to 4:30 – Friday – 8:30 to 1:30 – Saturday – 9 to 1...."

"You have to work on Saturdays?"

"Yea – at least I don't have to work on Sundays..."

"Thank God – I need to get my quality time in – and speaking of quality time... how soon will you be here?"

"I'm going to see Mommy..."

"Before you come home?"

"Yea..."

"Why won't you come home first?"

"Because... once I'm in your arms... I won't want to leave them..."

"Aww... I love you too..."

"I'm in Bridgeport now – I'll call you when I get there..."

"I'll come pick you up when you're ready to leave..."

"Okay – I love you..." I said as I hung up... "Shoot – I'm tired – I'm getting an Uber..." I said out loud as I order the Uber... "2 minutes – yes!" I said out loud. When he pulled up I checked the license plate but didn't get in right away...

"Starr?" the driver asked...

"Yes..." I answered and then I got in...

"Trumbull Garden's – right?"

"Yes…"

"You're pretty…"

"Thank you…"

"Can I ask you a question?"

"Sure…" I already knew where this was going…

"Are you seeing anyone right now?"

"As a matter-of-fact – I'm about to see my mother…" I laughed…

"Oh – you got jokes – okay…" he laughed… "I'ma give you a five-star rating for that – that was a good one…"

"Thank you – good night…" I said as I got out…

"You're welcome – I hope I get 5 stars…" he said as he drove off. I saw my mother watching the exchange…

"Hi Mommy…" I laughed as I hugged her…

"Hi Starr…" she laughed… "What's so funny?"

"He asked me if I was seeing anybody – I told him as a matter-of-fact I'm seeing my mother as soon as you drop me off…"

"Haaa… Haaa… - that's funny!"

"That's what he said…"

"You want something to drink?"

"Yes – a hot cup of tea…"

"Oh wow – you must have had some day…"

"Yes… I did…"

"Okay – I'll make us some tea…" My mother kept eyeing me while she was in the kitchen. She knew the conversation was going to be serious. I just sat there looking out the window until I heard the teakettle... "It'll be ready in a minute..." my mother said...

"Okay Mommy..." When my mother brought the tea to the table I didn't wait for it to cool off – I wrapped my hands around the mug and held it for a few minutes... and then I spoke... "Mommy?"

"Yes Starr..."

"I'm moving..."

"Is that what you needed to tell me?"

"Yea..."

"Starr – you're getting married – you're moving in with your husband – duh!" she laughed...

"No Mommy..."

"Wait – what? You're not moving in with Chandler?"

"Yes Mommy..."

"Starr?"

"Yes Mommy?"

"What's going on?"

"Beautiee talked to Daddy..."

"Oh... I see... when do I have to leave?"

"You don't..."

"I don't have to leave? Shit – I don't remember putting liquor in this tea!" she laughed...

"Mommy..."

"Yes Starr?"

"Beautiee got Daddy to help me…"

"Really?"

"Yes…"

"Oh – but not me – don't worry Starr – I'll be okay…"

"No Mommy – you can come too…"

"Pffffttt!" my mother spit tea out her mouth onto the table… "Wait a minute – Beautiee got your father – Bazil J. Osgood – to help you – and I can come?"

"Yea…"

"Shit –hold that thought – let me clean up this table – I gotta here this one…" she said as she got the cloth, cleaned the table, and sat down…

"Daddy bought me a co-op in Downtown Bridgeport…"

"Uh huh…"

"It's a one-bedroom corner unit…"

"Uh huh…"

"It's close to public transportation…"

"Uh huh…"

"It has coin-operated laundry in the basement…"

"Uh huh…"

"It's 9 minutes away from Chandler by car…"

"Uh huh…"

"Daddy paid for it in cash so I won't have a mortgage…"

"Uh huh…"

"The JOA fee, taxes, and insurance is less than $500 a month..."

"Uh huh..."

"And... Daddy said it's okay if you stay there..." My mother didn't say anything. We both finished our tea and then she spoke...

"Starr?"

"Yes Mommy?"

"What's the catch?"

"Daddy says... you have to sign a lease..." I sighed...

"Baby girl..." she laughed... "Are you telling me... your father... expects me... to pay him rent?"

"Yea..."

"Ahaaaa....! Ahaaaa....! Ahaaaa....!"

"Mommy – you can't stay unless you sign a lease and agree to pay rent..."

"Stop it... my stomach... I can't... Ahaaaa....! Ahaaaa....! Ahaaaa....!"

"Mommy... I'm serious..."

"You tell that Ratchet Bastard I said..." she said as she got up in my face... "He can subtract his rent from the child support he owes me for the last twenty-two years! Ahaaaa....! Ahaaaa....! Ahaaaa....!" I didn't say anything. I just sat there shaking my head... "And tell him I also said – if he has something to say to me – be a man – don't send a child to deliver his fuckin' messages! Ahaaaa....! Ahaaaa....! Ahaaaa....!"

"Hey Chan..." I answered...

"Is that your mother laughing in the background?"

"Yea..."

"You don't sound too happy..."

"I'm not..."

"I'm on my way..." Chandler said as he hurried downstairs, jumped in his car, put on the siren, and sped to Trumbull Gardens...

"Oh what – you're mad at me now?"

"Yes..."

"Oh well... that's too damn bad..."

"That's not right Mommy..."

"I'm not paying your father shit Starr!"

"Mommy – you're being really selfish!"

"Don't you dare talk to me like that!"

"Why not? You can call my father a Ratchet Bastard but I can't tell you you're being selfish?"

"Starr – it's Chandler – open the door..."

"You called the cops on me? You Lil' Bitch..."

"Mary – that's enough!" Chandler yelled as I jumped up to let him in...

"Mind your fuckin' business Chandler!"

"Starr is my business – and so are you – and you're not going to call her a Bitch again – not while I'm here..."

"What are you gonna do Sergeant? You gonna arrest me?"

"Mommy! Stop it!"

"Starr – let's go..." Chandler said...

"No!"

"Did you just tell me no?"

"Yes... I said no... I'm not leaving – not yet..." Chandler didn't say anything. He went to the table, pulled out a chair, and sat down... then I went in... "Mommy – you would be in a shelter right now if it wasn't for me!"

"You owe me! You wouldn't have Section 8 in the first place if it wasn't for me..."

"You're my mother! That's what you were supposed to do!"

"I went to jail Starr!"

"That's not on me! That's on you!"

"So what – I didn't suffer enough? Now you expect me to go down to welfare and get cash and food stamps? And pay your father rent?"

"You were fine with me going down to welfare when I lost my job – so why can't you go down to welfare?"

"I shouldn't have to go down to welfare – you have a job..."

'Mommy – I love you – and I'll help you – but it's not my job to take care of you..."

"Now who's being selfish?"

"You are Mommy!"

"How Starr? How am I being selfish?"

"The whole time you were in jail – I paid for everything when I was working – and when I lost my job – I struggled to pay for everything with my unemployment and food stamps – and I paid the phone bill too – and I never denied your calls – and now that you're out – I'm risking my Section 8 to keep you from going to a shelter – Beautiee talked to Daddy to help me because she knows I don't want you going to a shelter – and you don't thank me – you don't appreciate me – instead – you get mad and call me a Lil' Bitch because you have to pay rent!"

"You're right…" my mother sighed as she came over to me and pulled me into a hug… "I'm sorry…" she said as she started crying…

"I love you Mommy… you know that…"

"I know…"

"I have to go now Mommy – but I need you to be ready – Daddy says he's going to call me soon to sign papers…"

"Okay…"

"Good night Mommy…"

"Good night Starr…"

"Good night Mary…" Chandler said as he got up from the table…

"Good night Chandler…" my mother said as we left and she closed the door…

"You okay?" Chandler asked…

"Yea…"

"No you're not – c'mere…" he said as he pulled me into a hug…

"I'm glad you were here…"

"I'm glad I was too…"

"She hurt my feelings…"

"I know she did…"

"Was I wrong?"

"Do you think you were wrong?"

"No..."

"Neither do I..."

"My father won't like this..."

"You don't have to tell him..."

"She didn't have to say what she said either..."

"You're right..." Chandler said as he opened the car door for me and I got in. Chandler closed the door, went to the driver's side, got in, closed the door, and took my hand... "Starr..."

"Yes Chandler?"

"I hate that you're in the middle of this..."

"So do I..."

"I'ma put a stop to it..."

"Chandler..."

"I don't care what you say Starr – you're going to be my wife – I'm not having it – you understand me?" I didn't answer him. I moved closer to him, threw my arms around him, and kissed him deeply. Chandler held me and we continued kissing for a few moments... "Are you hungry?"

"Yes..."

"I made dinner..." he said as he started the car...

"Good – I'm tired..."

"Too tired for dessert?" he asked as we drove off...

"Not that tired..." I laughed...

"Good..." Chandler said as he looked at me mischeviously. We didn't speak the rest of the way home. When we got home, Chandler parked the car, we got out, and went upstairs. Chandler was all over me as soon as we closed the door... "Congratulations..." he said as he started unbuttoning my blouse and slid it off my shoulders...

"For what?" I asked as I started unbuckling his belt, unzipped his pants, and slid them off his ass along with his boxers to the floor...

"Your first day at work..." he said as he pulled me to him, ran his hands up my back, unclasped my bra, and took it off...

"Thank you..." I said as I ripped his shirt open, popping the buttons, and slid it off his shoulders...

"You're welcome..." he said as he pulled me by my waist, unzipped my pants, and slid them off my ass along with my panties to the floor. I lifted Chandler's t-shirt over his head and instead of putting his arms back down he pulled me to him and started kissing me on my neck while walking me backwards towards the couch. I held on to him as he laid me down on the couch, climbed on top of me, and eased himself inside me...

"Chandler..." I moaned as he began thrusting...

"Yes... Starr..." I wrapped my legs around his back and locked my feet to pull him in deeper as he put his tongue in my mouth and kissed me hard...

"Mmmm..... Mmmm... Mmmm..."

"Mmmph...   Mmmph...   Mmmph... Mmmph..."

"Mmmm..... Mmmm... Mmmm..."

"Mmmph...   Mmmph...   Mmmph... Mmmph..."

"Mmmm..... Mmmm... Mmmm..."

"Mmmph...   Mmmph...   Mmmph... Mmmph..." I dug my nails into Chandler's back and bit his shoulder as I got closer to cumming...

"Huuhhh....   Huuhhh...   Huuhhhh... Huuhhh..."

"Mmmph...   Mmmph...   Mmmph... Mmmph..." Chandler moaned in my ear...

"Huuhhh....   Huuhhh...   Huuhhhh... Huuhhh..."

"Mmmph...   Mmmph...   Mmmph... Mmmph..." I dug my nails into the small of his back as I came hard...

"Haahhh....   Haahhh...   Haahhhh... Haahhh..."

"Mmmph...   Mmmph...   Mmmph... Mmmph..."

"Chandler..." I breathed...

"Starr... Damn..."

"That was good..."

"Yes... it was..."

"I love this couch..."

"I love this couch too..." We started kissing and I continued holding him down on top of me... "Starr..." Chandler said between kisses... "Let... Me... Feed... You..."

"Mmmm... okay..."

"Starr... let... me... go..."

"Never..."

"Okay..." Chandler said as he pulled me up off the couch with my arms still around his neck. Chandler held me by my waist as he walked me backwards towards the kitchen table and sat me in the chair... "I thought you said you'd never let me go..." he laughed...

"I can't hold you while I eat... at least not yet..." I laughed... Chandler went to get plates out the cabinet and I admired his ass as he put salad, steak, and butter noodles on each plate, brought them to the table, and sat down. We looked at our clothes in the living room on the floor, we looked back at each other, and started eating...

"Since you get off at 1:30 on Friday – I want us to go get our marriage license..."

"Okay..."

"When you fill it out, they ask for the name of your parents, your maiden name, and you fill in your married name..."

"What's your last name"

"Corbett..."

"Hmm... Starr Corbett..."

"Sounds good…"

"Chandler?"

"Yes Starr?"

"Can I keep my maiden name?"

"You don't like my name?"

"I love your name… it's just…"

"What?"

"It's silly… never mind…"

"Starr… tell me…"

"I just found my father…"

"Starr – he's always gonna be your father – no matter what your name is…"

"I know… but…"

"So you're gonna marry me – and be Mrs. Osgood?'

"No… I wanna be Mrs. Corbett – I just want to keep my father's name too…"

"You can be Starr Osgood Corbett if you want…"

"You're not mad?"

"We're getting married…" Chandler said as he finished his food…"

"I love you Chandler…"

"Finish your food…" he said as he opened the refrigerator, took out a bottle of white wine, took two wine glassed from the cabinet, and walked towards the bedroom. I sat there eating and my phone started ringing… "Starr – is that your phone?"

"Yea…" I answered as I finished my food…

"You gonna answer it?" I didn't answer him. I got up from the table, picked up my phone, turned it off, connected it to the charger, and went into the bedroom. Chandler was sitting up in bed drinking wine and when he saw me he held up a glass of wine for me. I went over to the bed, took the glass of wine, took and sip, and climbed in beside him...

"How'd you get this number?" Bazil asked...

"I took it out your daughter's phone..."

"Why are you calling Mary?"

"Listen to me and listen good you Ratchet Bastard – I'm not signing a fuckin' lease – and I'm not paying you any got damn rent!"

"Is that right?"

"That's right – and another thing..."

"Yes Mary?"

"The next time you have something to say to me – be a man – don't send a lil' girl to deliver your messages..."

"Now that I have your number I'll be sure to deliver any messages I have for you personally – and Mary?"

"Yea?"

"I want to thank you..."

"For what?"

"For giving me the opportunity to remind you – once again – who the fuck you're dealing with... good night... I'll see you soon..."

"What the fuck is that supposed to mean?"

"I'll be sure to deliver the message to you... personally..." he said as he hung up...

"Who was that?" Beautiee asked...

"It was Mary..." Bazil laughed...

"Why is she calling you?" Beautiee as she sat up...

"Beautiee..." Bazil said as he climbed in bed beside her and kissed her... "You have nothing to worry about..." he said as he pulled her down onto her back, climbed on top of her, and eased himself inside her...

"You promise?" Beautiee asked as Bazil held her and began thrusting...

"Yes... Beautiee... I... promise... you... have... nothing... to... worry... about..."

"Good..." she breathed...

"Is it? Is it good?"

"Yes... Oh God Bazil... Yes..."

Chapter 7

"Who is it?" Mary asked as she heard knocking...

"Housing..."

"I'll be right there... hang on..." Mary said as she put on her robe and went to the door... "May I help you?" she asked as she looked out the peep hole and saw two men...

"Is Starr Osgood Home?"

"She's not here at the moment..."

"Okay – thank you..." the man said. Mary started to walk away from the door and noticed an envelope had been slipped underneath...

"Hmmm..." Mary said as she picked up the envelope... "It's not sealed... let me see what this is – it might be important..." she said as she opened the envelope, took the letter out, and began reading...

NOTICE OF EVICTION

Dear Ms. Osgood,

It has been brought to our attention that you have someone living in your apartment that has a felony. This is a direct violation of your housing agreement, as well as your Section 8 Certificate.

You have 72 hours from the date on this letter – Tuesday, May 21st, 2019 – to remove this tenant or face eviction. On Friday, May 24th, 2019, we will be at your apartment at 4:30 p.m. sharp to do an inspection. Failure to adhere to these instructions will result in eviction and report to HUD for violating your Section 8.

"Shit! Shit! Shit! Shit! Shit!" Mary cursed out loud… "What the fuck am I gonna do? I can't let Starr get evicted – I gotta get the fuck outta here…

"Hello Starr – listen…" she said as she answered her phone…

"It's Bazil…"

"What the hell do you want?"

"Did you get my message?"

"Mutha fucka!"

'I'll take that as a yes… you have a good day… and good luck…" Bazil laughed as Mary hung up…

"I guess I need to call Starr – dammit – I was so fuckin' stupid – oh well..." she said as she tried to call Starr... "Hmmm... straight to voice mail – she probably has to turn her phone off at work – I'll try to get her later on... sigh... I may as well make myself a cup of coffee..." she said as she went into the kitchen...

"Good morning Ms. Crystal..." I answered...

"How'd you know it was me?"

"I have your number stored in my phone..."

"Are you in the middle of something? I can call you back..."

"It's okay Ms. Crystal – I can talk a minute – I'm just busy with work..."

"You have a job?"

"Yes Ms. Crystal..."

"Congratulations – when did you start?"

"Yesterday was my first day..."

"I need to see you as soon as possible..."

"Is something wrong Ms. Crystal?"

"I got a copy of the letter you received from housing..."

"I didn't get a letter..."

"That's because you're at work – did you talk to your mother?"

"Not since yesterday..."

"She probably got the letter this morning..."

"What letter?"

"Starr... you got an eviction notice..."

"Oh my God... How much time do I have?"

"If your mother leaves – you won't get evicted... but she has to be gone by Friday..."

"Okay – I can come see you Friday afternoon..."

"They're inspecting your apartment at 4:30 p.m. – you need to be home – I need to see you before that..."

"Okay... I'll be there..." I said as I hung up...

"You okay Starr?" my supervisor, Amy Hurley, asked...

"Not really..."

"You need to leave?"

"Yea..."

"If I let you leave... will you be back?"

"Ms. Hurley?"

"Yes Starr?"

"I love this job – I'll be back... I promise..."

"Oh thank God!"

"You're welcome..." God said...

"I'll call you later Ms. Hurley..."

"Okay Honey... see you later..." she said as I left to get the train...

"I'm going to see Chandler – and we're going to get our marriage license..." I said out loud on my way to the train station... "Let's see – the next train is as 12:21 and I'll get to Bridgeport at 12:45 – perfect..." I said as I started running... "Whew!" Made it! Good thing I have this app so I can buy my ticket on my phone..." I bought my ticket just in time...

"Ticket please..." the conductor said as soon as I bought the ticket. I couldn't wait to get to Chandler. As soon as I got to Bridgeport I got off the train and went straight to the precinct...

"Hey Starr..." the officers said as soon as I walked into the main area...

"Starr..." Chandler said as he walked up to me... "What are you doing here?"

"Can we get out of here?"

"Sure..." Chandler said as he put his arm around me... Let's go..." and we walked out the precinct... "Starr?"

"Yes Chandler?'

"C'mere..." he said as he pulled me into a hug and held me... and I started crying...

"Can we go to City Hall and get our marriage license?"

"Right now?"

"Yes..."

"If that's what you want..." he said and then he kissed me...

"That's what I want..."

"Okay..." Chandler said as we went to the car. Chandler opened the door for me and helped me in, then he got in himself, and we went straight to City Hall.

"Good afternoon..." the clerk said... "How may I help you?"

"We're here to get our marriage license..." I said as I smiled...

"Aww... congratulations..."

"Thank you..."

"Do you have valid identification?"

"What do you mean?"

"If you have identification from the Department of Motor Vehicles that'll be sufficient – otherwise, I'll need another form of identification and your birth certificate..."

"We have valid identification..." Chandler said as he showed the clerk his badge...

"That sure is a pretty badge... Sergeant..." the clerk said as she smiled.

"Here..." Chandler said as he handed the clerk his driver's license...

"May I have your ID please?" she asked me...

"Sure..." I said as I handed her my license...

"I need to make a copy of these to attach to your application – I'll be right back..." she said as she walked over to the copy machine. Chandler and I looked at each other and smiled...

"Here ya go..." the clerk said as she gave us back our licenses...

"I need you both to fill this out completely – once you fill it out – I'll look it over, make sure it's filled out properly, and then we'll all sign it..."

"Okay..." Chandler said as he took the form and began filling it out. I waited patiently as he filled out his side, but I wanted him to hurry up so I could fill out mine...

"Here, here!" Chandler laughed as he gave it to me. I studied his side and then started filling out my side with my name, date of birth, social security number, etc., and then I filled in my parent's information: Mother – Mary Smith, Father – Bazil J. Osgood. I went down the rest of the form and compared my answers to Chandlers: City of Birth – Bridgeport, State – CT, Prior Marriages – No, Maiden Name – Starr Osgood, Name on Marriage Certificate – I got another piece of paper and wrote two names: Starr Corbett, Starr Osgood Corbett...

"I like this one..." I said as I wrote Starr Osgood Corbett on the form. After I filled in the name to be put on the Marriage Certificate I checked 'no' where they asked for preference to hyphenate the name. I saw Chandler's signature at the bottom of the form and I started crying after I signed my name...

"Aww..." the clerk said as she handed me tissues...

"Sorry..." I laughed...

"Don't ever apologize for happiness..." she said as she took the form and read it over...

"Chandler?" she asked...

"Yes?"

"Did you fill this out of your own free will?"

"Yes Maam..."

"Is this your signature?" she asked as she pointed to his signature...

"Yes Maam..."

"Starr?"

"Yes?"

"Did you fill this out of your own free will?"

"Yes Maam!"

"Is this your signature?" she asked as she pointed to my signature...

"Yes Maam!"

"Okay..." she laughed... "Wait a minute..."

"What's wrong?" I asked...

"Bazil Osgood... he's your father?"

"Yes Maam!"

"Oh wow..."

"You know my father?"

"Everybody knows your father..."

"Is that good or bad?" I asked...

"Its fine sweetheart..." she said as she signed the form. "I'm going to process this and get you your license – once I do that – you can get married anytime you want – but you have to get married within 60 days – if you don't get married in 60 days, it will expire – and you'll be back to see me... I'll be right back..." she said as she went into the office behind the counter...

"I love you Chandler..."

"I love you too..." Chandler said and then he kissed me...

"Here's your license..." the clerk said as she handed us our license. We looked at the license, and then we looked at each other...

"Do you have any questions?" I looked at our license again and read the signature at the bottom:

Prepared by: Alberta Woody

Title: City Clerk

City: Bridgeport

State: CT

"No..." I sighed...

"Do you have any questions Chandler?"

"No Maam..."

"On your wedding day – give this license to the wedding officiant – they'll sign it, date it, and then they'll mail it out to Vital Records for the state you get married in and a copy of it will also be sent here. You'll receive your Marriage Certificate from the Vital Records Office..."

"Thank you Ms. Woody..." I said as I gave her a hug..."

"You can call me Alberta..." she said as she pulled us both into a hug and started crying...

"You okay?" Chandler asked...

"I'm fine – I'm just happy..." she said as she wiped her eyes..."

"Aww... we're happy too... right Starr?"

"Yes sir!" I yelled so loud everyone in the office bust out laughing.

"I'm getting married!" I yelled from the top of the steps as soon as we stepped outside.

People in the street stopped and applauded while we held each other and kissed. Some of the officers recognized Chandler...

"Yea Sarge! Woo hoo!" they yelled as they applauded. We were blocking the entrance but everyone was happy for us so they just waited until we stopped kissing...

"I'm so happy..." I cried...

"This... this right here... as long as you're happy... you can cry all you want..." Chandler said as he continued to hold me...

"Do you have to go back to work?"

"Not if you don't want me to..."

"I don't want you to..."

"Okay – Thompson – I'm out for the rest of the day!"

"Okay – see you tomorrow..."

"Let's go to Thelma's"

"Okay Chandler..." I said as we held hands walking down the stairs. We walked hand-in-hand to Thelma's went inside, got a table and sat down...

"Welcome to Thelma's – do you need to see a menu?"

"Yes Maam..." Chandler said...

"Would you like something to drink?"

"I'd like a sweet tea..."

"Make that two..." I said.

"You have a pretty smile..." she said as she looked at me..."

"Thank you..."

"Is he responsible for that smile?"

"Yes... he is..."

"Do you have any brothers? I haven't smiled like that in years..." she laughed...

"I don't have any brothers – but I have a few friends at the precinct that might be interested in making you smile..." Chandler answered...

"Aww... you're sweet – let me go get your tea..." she said as she walked away...

"Starr?"

"Yes Chandler?"

"Tell me..."

"Sigh... I just wanna be happy..."

"I'll take care of that..."

"You already are..."

"Tell me... please..." I got up from the right side of the booth and went to sit on the left side of the booth beside Chandler. I didn't say anything – I just laid my head on his shoulder and Chandler put his arm around me...

"Here's your tea – have you had a chance to look at the menu?" the waitress asked...

"I already know what I want..." Chandler said...

"What can I get you – besides her..." she laughed, pointing at me...

"I'll have some smothered pork chops with baked macaroni & cheese, and collard greens – seasoned with turkey..."

"I see you have what you want already..." she laughed... "but what can I get you to eat Maam?" she asked me...

"Hmmm... I'll have the party wings with potato salad and candied yams..."

"Okay... I'll be back..." she said as she picked up the menus and went to place our orders...

"I'm getting evicted Chandler..."

"Starr... when do you have to be out?"

"I have 72 hours to put my mother out... or I get evicted..."

"When did you find out about this?"

"This morning..."

"Your mother called you?"

"No – Ms. Crystal called me..."

"Who's that?"

"Ms. Cox..."

"Ohh... how did she know?"

"They served her a copy of my notice of eviction..." I sighed...

"I'm sorry..."

"So am I Chandler..."

"What are you going to do?"

"Ms. Crystal needs to see me on Friday..."

"Okay..."

"Housing is coming to do an inspection on Friday afternoon to make sure my mother's gone..."

"What time?"

"4:30..."

"Okay – do you want me to be there with you?"

"No..."

"You sure?"

"Yea..."

"So your mother's going to have to go to the shelter?"

"Yea..."

"Starr?"

"Yes Chandler?"

"I have 3 bedrooms..."

"I know..."

"Your mother can come stay with us if you don't want her to go to the shelter..."

"I love you Chandler..."

"I love you too..."

"My mother has to go to the shelter..."

"Are you sure? I don't mind..."

"I mind..."

"Starr..."

"No Chandler..."

"Okay..."

"My father said we'll be closing soon on my co-op – if my mother still doesn't want to sign the lease and pay rent, then she can stay in the shelter – it's up to her – as for me – I'm getting married – and I can't be myself and walk around in your shirts or make love to you in the living room with my mother in the house..." I laughed...

"True dat..." Chandler laughed... "I just want to make sure you're okay..."

"I'm fine Chandler – I'ma a Lil' Bitch remember?'

"Starr!"

"What?" I answered as I finished my tea...

"Here's your food..." the waitress interrupted... "Can I get you some more tea?"

"Yes Maam!" I answered...

"I'll be right back..." she said as she went to get more tea and came back with a pitcher...

"Just leave the pitcher here..." I laughed...

"Okay..." the waitress laughed...

"Give me your hand Starr..." Chandler said...

"Okay..."

"Lord, thank you for this food... this drink... and my wife... Amen..."

"Amen! I yelled...

"You're in a mood..."

"Wait 'till you get me home..." I said as I smiled mischievously...

"Aww shit!" Chandler laughed... "It's on – ain't it?"

"Damn sure is!" I laughed as we ate...

"You sure you're okay?"

"Chandler?"

"Yes Starr?"

"Let's pick a date..."

"Right now?"

"Yes... now..."

"Okay – it's too close to Memorial Day – so how about June?"

"June is filled with proms and graduations…"

"What's that got to do with us?"

"Well…" I answered as I filled my glass again… "places will be booked… and crowded…"

"True dat…" I took out my phone and started looking up cruises… "What are you doing Starr?"

"Hang on a second…"

"Okay…" Chandler said as he poured himself some more tea…"

"Let's get married Wednesday, July 17th…"

"Hmm… why not get married on Saturday, July 20th?"

"Because – I just found a 4-night cruise going to Bermuda – and it leaves Boston on Thursday, July 18th – and returns on Monday, July 22nd – and the next cruise going to Bermuda isn't leaving until September…"

"That's cutting it pretty close – see if you can find one in June…"

"Okay… hold on…" I said as I went back to my phone… "I found a 7 might cruise – it leaves Boston on Friday, June 7th – and returns on Friday, June 14th at 8:00 a.m…."

"I like that one better – I don't have to wait so long to marry you…"

"Aww… I love you…"

"Plus… our honeymoon is longer…" he said as he smiled at me mischievously…

"So we're getting married on Thursday, June 6th?'

"Yes..."

"Since we're going on a cruise... can we get married at a Bed & Breakfast?"

"Starr... we can get married anywhere you want... as long as you're my wife when we're done..."

"Okay... I just did a search for wedding venues in Boston... and I like the Taylor House Bed & Breakfast..." I said as I showed him the picture...

"I like it..."

"It looks so romantic..."

"It does..."

"It says it's in Boston's Jamaica Plain neighborhood..."

"Starr?"

"Yes Chandler?"

"Book it..."

"Okay..." I sighed...

"Are you ready for your check?' the waitress asked...

"Yes Maam..." Chandler answered...

"Here ya go..." she said as she placed the check on the table...

"And here you go..." Chandler said as he placed the check in her hand along with a $50 bill...

"Can we go see my father?" I asked...

"If you want to..."

"You don't want to?"

"Not really…"

"Okay…" I sighed…

"No it's not – you said you wanted to be happy – right?"

"Yes…"

"If we go see your father – will that make you happy?"

"Yes…" I answered with a smile…

"Let's go then…" Chandler said as we got up and left.

Chapter 8

"Hi Daddy…"

"Hi Starr…"

"We're coming to see you…"

"I guess you wanna talk about your mother…"

"Yea…"

"Sigh… okay – we'll see you soon…"

"What's wrong?" Beautiee asked…

"Starr's coming…"

"You don't want to see her?"

"I love her – I'm just not looking forward to our conversation…" he sighed…

"Maybe Sheddi will call us soon and we'll be able to close – then Starr can help her mother…"

"Beautiee…"

"Yes Bazil?"

"I need to tell you something…"

"Come here Bazil…" Bazil walked over to Beautiee and stood in front of her… "Yes Beautiee?"

"I need to hold you..." she said as she opened her arms...

"I love you..." Bazil said as they held each other...

"I love you too..."

"Beautiee... I need to tell you..."

"Ssshhh..." Beautiee said as she put her head on his chest. Bazil stood still and let Beautiee hold him as he held her...

"What are you doing?" he whispered...

"I'm listening to your heart..." she whispered...

"I love you..."

"I love you too..."

"I need to tell you something..."

"Okay Bazil..." she said as she sat down on the couch... "Tell me..." Bazil sat down next to Beautiee and took her hands... "Please don't tell Starr..."

"Okay..."

"When Mary called me the other night... she told me she wasn't signing a lease and she wasn't paying any rent..."

"Okay..."

"What should I do?"

"Nothing..."

"Nothing?"

"Nothing..."

"Okay..."

"Come here..." Bazil moved closer to Beautiee and she pulled him into a kiss. Bazil wrapped his arms around her, held her, and they continued kissing until we knocked on the door...

"Who is it?" my father asked...

"Me Daddy..."

"I'll be right there..." my father said as he got up to let us in...

"Daddy!"

"Hi Starr..."

"Daddy!" Chandler laughed as he pulled my father into a hug..."

"Hello son..." my father laughed...

"Starr.... Come say hello to your lil' brother..." Beautiee said as she came towards me with open arms...

"Hi lil' brother..." I said as I hugged her... "Hi Beautiee..."

"Hi Starr..."

"Oh my goodness... calm down lil' brother..." I laughed...

"He's been active all day..."

"Hmm... maybe he knew I was coming..."

"Chandler – come say hello to your lil' brother-in-law..."

"Hi lil' brother-in-law..." Chandler laughed... "This is too funny..."

"It is..." Beautiee laughed...

"Starr?"

"Yes Beautiee?"

"When your mother was pregnant with you – did you come early?"

"I don't know – why?"

"I think your lil' brother will be here soon..."

"What's wrong Beautiee?" my father asked as he came in the foyer...

"I think your son is coming sooner rather than later..."

"Oh my God – do we need to go to the hospital?"

"No Bazil – not today – but soon..."

"Let's go in the living room – we have lot to tell you..." I said...

"Okay Starr..." Beautiee said as we all went into the living room and sat down...

"I got a call from Ms. Cox today..."

"Who's Ms. Cox?" Beautiee asked...

"My caseworker from Section 8..."

"Is everything okay?" My father asked...

"No Daddy..."

"What's wrong?'

"Ms. Cox was served with a copy of my eviction notice..."

"Oh my God!" Beautiee said...

"I have 72 hours to get my mother out of my apartment or I get evicted..."

"So she has to be out by Friday..." my father said...

"Yes Daddy..."

"I'm sorry Starr..."

"It's okay Daddy..."

"Maybe we'll hear from Sheddi soon..." Beautiee said...

"What are you going to do Starr?" my father asked...

"I'm getting married Daddy!"

"I know..." my father laughed...

"Daddy... you don't understand..."

"Go ahead Starr..."

"Housing is coming on Friday to make sure Mommy's out of the apartment – and I also have to go see Ms. Cox..."

"Okay..."

"So Chandler and I were supposed to go to City Hall on Friday to get our marriage license..."

"Okay..."

"And I didn't want to wait anymore..."

"What are you saying Starr?"

"We have our marriage license Daddy! We're getting married!" I cried...

"Starr..." my father whispered as he started to cry...

"Congratulations!" Beautiee said...

"We set a date..." Chandler said...

"Already?" my father asked...

"Yes Daddy..."

"We're getting married on Thursday, June 6th at the Taylor House Bed & Breakfast in Boston..." Chandler said...

"I thought you were getting married in church?" Beautiee asked...

"We were... but our cruise to Bermuda leaves Boston on Friday, June 7th and returns on Friday, June 14th..." Chandler said...

"I love it – Starr – if you need anything..." Beautiee said...

"Yes! I need everything!" I laughed...

"C'mon Starr – let's go into the library and get this booked..." I laughed...

"Starr?" my father asked...

"Yes Daddy?"

"What are you going to do about your mother?"

"Daddy?"

"Yes Starr..."

"Mommy told me she wasn't signing the lease and she wasn't paying rent – so Mommy has to go to the shelter..."

"Really?" my father asked...

"Mommy has to be out by Friday and you haven't heard from the real estate agent yet – either way – Mommy has to go to the shelter – maybe she'll change her mind after she's been in the shelter for a few days – c'mon Beautiee..." I said as we went into the library...

Chapter 9

"Thank you..." Bazil said to Chandler...

"For what?"

"I don't know what you did... or what's gotten into her... but thank you..."

"You're welcome..."

"Did you have anything to do with Starr's decision?" Chandler bust out laughing...

"What's so funny?"

"I have 3 bedrooms..."

"Okay..."

"I told Starr her mother could stay with us if she wanted..."

"Oh wow... what'd she say?"

"Man-to-man?"

"Man-to-man..."

"Starr said she can't walk around the house in my shirt, be herself, or make love to me with her mother in the house..."

"I see..." Bazil said...

"Beautiee?"

"Yes Starr?"

"We had a fight…"

"Who?"

"Me and my mother…"

"What happened?"

"I told my mother Daddy said she could stay if she signs a lease and pays rent but she said she wasn't doing that…"

"I know…"

"You know?"

"Don't tell your father I told you…"

"Okay…"

"Your mother called your father last night…"

"Beautiee?"

"Yes Starr…"

"It was bad…"

"What happened?"

"Chandler heard us arguing when he banged on the door…"

"Oh wow…"

"I let him in and she thought I called the police on her…"

"Oh my God…"

"She called Daddy a Ratchet Bastard…"

"What?!"

"Chandler was really mad…"

"I'm starting to get mad…"

"Please don't tell Daddy…"

"I won't…"

"She called me a Lil' Bitch…" I said as I started crying…

"Oh Starr..." Beautiee said as she hugged me... "I'm so sorry... you didn't deserve that..."

"I love her so much..."

"She didn't mean it Starr..."

"Really?"

"She's just mad at your father..."

"I know she's mad at my father – but I hope she changes her mind..."

"Me too – especially since we're planning your wedding – I need her help!"

"You do?"

"Of course – we have to get you booked, get your passports – get you a wedding dress – we can't do all that without your mother – your lil' brother doesn't let me stay on my feet for too long..." Beautiee laughed... "Okay – the first thing we need to do is book the Taylor Bed & Breakfast..." she said as she looked it up on the computer... "Hang on..." she said as she dialed their number...

"Thank you for calling Taylor House Bed & Breakfast – this is Darryl..."

"Hello Darryl – this is Mrs. Osgood..."

"Hello Mrs. Osgood – how may I help you?"

"My daughter's getting married on Thursday, June 6th..."

"Congratulations!"

"Thank you..."

"Would you like to have the ceremony here?"

"Yes..."

"Okay – this is barely two weeks' notice – we normally require a minimum of 10 people for the reception..."

"That's fine..."

"Okay – on our website I want you to go to the estimate page..."

"Okay – come take a look Starr..."

"Okay..." Beautiee said as she filled in everything on the page from the guest count, event day, season, cocktail hour, menu type, beverage package, and all the services..."

"I'm so happy you can do all this..." Beautiee said...

"No problem at all Mrs. Osgood – we have three rooms available on June 6th for overnight – I'll describe each room..."

"We'll take all three..." Beautiee said...

"Okay – great – now do you see the estimate below at the bottom?"

"Yes I do..."

"I need to tell you that it's just an estimate – pricing could go up or down depending on whether you upgrade and it's subject to change..."

"That's fine – I'll take it – if it goes up – we'll make the adjustments – if it goes down – you'll make the adjustments..." Beautiee laughed...

"Okay – will that be cash, check, or charge?"

"Starr – bring me my pocket book..."

"Okay..." I said as I got up to get her pocketbook and bring it to her..."

"It'll be charge... here's my card number..." I watched and waited until Beautiee finished...

"You're all set – the time, instructions, check-inn, etc., will be forwarded to you – just call if you have any questions – what's your email?"

"beautiee@beautifulpublications.com   - Starr - what's your email?"

"sOsgood@gmail.com..."

"Could you also cc sOsgood@gmail.com?"

"Sure..."

"Thank you..."

"You're welcome Mrs. Osgood – you'll hear from us shortly..."

"Okay – now we need to get your cruise booked so you can go on your honeymoon... Starr? What's wrong?"

"I love you..." I cried...

"Aww... I love you too Starr..." she said as she pulled me into a hug... "Now – let's get you booked on your cruise..." she said as she pulled up the search for cruises leaving Boston... "Here we go – Norwegian Cruiseline – is this the one you wanted?"

"Yes..."

"Do you want an inside, ocean view, balcony, or suite?"

"The suites are expensive – inside the room is fine..."

"Starr?"

"Yes Beautiee?"

"Do you want a suite?"

"Yea..."

"Here – look at this..."

"Okay..."

"It says your view from the balcony may be fully obstructed or partially obstructed – oh Starr – look at the penthouse!"

"It says its' perfect for a romantic get away..." I sighed...

"And it includes butler and concierge service..."

"They're both so nice..."

"Do you want the aft-facing or the forward facing?"

"I should get Chandler and see what he wants..." I said as I started to get up...

"Starr?"

"Yes Beautiee?"

"Surprise him..."

"Okay... I'll take the aft-facing penthouse..."

"Good – I like that one too..."

"This is confusing..."

"Starr – see where those lights ae blinking?"

"Yes..."

"Those are the available rooms..."

"Ohh... okay... I'll take 8630 – the one on the end..."

"Okay... now we just fill in the name of the passengers, booking contact person, queen bed, and we'll fill in that you're celebrating your anniversary..."

"We're newlyweds..." I laughed...

"Doesn't matter – we're done!"

"Do we need passports?"

"Yes – you need to make an appointment at the Connecticut passport Agency in Stamford – you're traveling within 14 days so you can get it expedited..."

"Thank you so much!" I said as I hugged her tight...

"You're welcome Starr – now we need to get your mother on board..."

"I wish we could..."

"Why can't we?"

"She has to go to the shelter on Friday..."

"Starr?"

"Yes Beautiee?"

"That doesn't mean we can't pick her up and drop her off..."

"You'll do that?'

"Sure... unless you wanna take the bus..." Beautiee laughed...

"Where are we going?"

"Well... you need a dress – David's Bridal is your best bet for wedding dresses on short notice – they always have dresses on sale and you can get your tierra and shoes there too..."

"I have so much to do..."

"Yes you do – but I'll help you every step of the way – as long as your brother doesn't' mind..." Beautiee laughed...

"I have to tell Chandler – I have to tell my job – I have to get my passport..."

"What are your hours at work?"

"Monday through Thursday I work 8:30 to 4:30 – Friday I work 8:30 to 1:30 – Saturday I work 9 to 1..."

"Okay – we'll go dress shopping on Saturday..."

"Okay – Chandler – I have so much to tell you!" I yelled as I ran into the living room...

"You still happy right?"

"Yes Chandler..." I said as I smiled...

"Good – you can fill me in when we get home..." Chandler said as he got up... "And Beautiee?"

"Yes Chndler..."

"Le'me know how much I owe you..."

"Nothing..." my father said...

"Okay – thank you – but le'me get the honeymoon..."

"Okay – my father said...

"Good night Daddy – I love you..." I said as we hugged...

"Good night Starr – I love you too..."

"Good night Beautiee – good night lil' brother – I'll see you Saturday..." I said as we hugged.

"See you Saturday..." Beautiee said...

"Good night Chandler..." my father said as he pulled Chandler into a hug...

"Good night Bazil..." Chandler said...

"Bring it here Chandler..." Beautiee said as she held out her arms waiting for a hug..."

"Good night Beautiee..." Chandler said as they hugged...

"Good night..." she said as we left... "Whew! I'm tired..."

"Are you Okay?"

"Yes Bazil – I'm fine..."

"So... Saturday?"

"Yea..."

"How much are we in for... so far?"

"Ten thousand... so far...."

"What's happening on Saturday?"

"We're going shopping for dresses..."

"You and Starr?"

"And Mary..."

"Hmmm... interesting..."

"She's worried about her mother..."

"I know..."

"I told her I need her mother's help..."

"I love you..." Bazil said and then he kissed her..."

"Mmmm... I love you too..."

"Hungry?"

"Always..."

"What can I get you?"

"I've been thinking..."

"Yes?" Bazil asked as he started kissing her neck...

"I haven't quenched my thirst in a while..."

"You're right..." he breathed as he continued kissing her neck...

"I think I'd like to quench my thirst..."

"Okay... if that's what you want..."

"That's what I want..."

"Where?" Bazil asked as he pulled her close and kissed her...

"In the living room..."

"On the couch?"

"Yea..."

"Come with me..." he said as he took her back into the living room and sat her down on the couch. Beautiee watched as Bazil did a strip tease from the bottom down. He started with his belt, took it off, and danced with it before tossing it to the floor. He put his hands on his waist, unzipped his pants slowly and deliberately, and let them fall along with his boxers of his ass to his knees, and then to the floor as he twisted and swerved. He stepped out of them and strolled over to Beautiee, picked up her face by her chin, and looked in her eyes. He took his dick in his hands and started stroking it in front of her as he inched closer to her mouth... "You want this?" he asked...

"Yes... I want that..." Beautiee breathed...

"How thirsty are you?"

"Very..."

"Show me..." Beautiee moved to the edge of the couch, grabbed Bazil by his ass, opened her mouth, and took Bazil's dick in her mouth all the way down to his balls... "Shit... Beautiee..." Beautiee kept one hand on Bazil's ass and began stroking his dick from the base with her other hand while simultaneously sucking the head of his dick... "Oohhh... Shit..." Beautiee took Bazil's dick in her mouth again all the way down to his balls, slurping and sucking as she did so... "Got damn Beautiee... Shit!" Beautiee pushed Bazil by his ass into her mouth down the back of her throat and deep throated him for a few moments... "Beautiee! Fuck!" Bazil said as he grabbed the sides of her head and played with her hair. Beautiee's sucking and slurping got sloppier as Bazil fucked her mouth and she felt his legs trembling... "I'm gonna cum in your mouth... uuuggghhh... Fuuuccckkk!" Beautiee swallowed every drop and continued sucking softly as long as Bazil allowed her to. She felt him getting hard again in her mouth and started stroking his dick from the base as she continued sucking... "Damn your mouth feels good..." he breathed as he grabbed her head on both sides and started fucking her mouth again. Beautiee relaxed her jaws and continued sucking at a slow, steady pace until she felt his legs trembling again and then she grabbed his ass with her hands and picked up the pace... "Beautiee... suck it... shit... I'm cumming again... Fuck... Aaaahhhhh!"

Beautiee swallowed and continued sucking him softly until he tapped her on the shoulder... "Beautiee... he whispered...

"Yes... My Thirst Quencher..." she whispered and then she put his dick back in her mouth...

"Still thirsty?"

"Mmmm Hmmm..." she moaned with his dick still in her mouth...

"Come here..." Beautiee stood up and faced Bazil...

"Yes... My Thirst Quencher?"

"I... love... you..." he said in between kisses...

"Mmmm... I... love... you... too..."

"I missed your mouth..."

"Aww... I'm sorry... I'll make it up to you..."

"You just did..."

"You want more?"

"Yes... please..."

"Okay... let's go upstairs... and I'll give your more..."

"Okay..." Bazil said as they went upstairs to the bedroom. Beautiee sat on the bed and propped herself up against the headboard...

"Come here My Thirst Quencher..." Bazil climbed up on the bed and straddled himself over Beautiee in front of her face. Beautiee took Bazil's dick in her mouth again and grabbed

Bazil's ass and pushed him further into her mouth...

"Beautiee... shit... suck it... fuck... your mouth..." Beautiee began swirling her tongue around his dick and continued sucking... "Beautiee... ooohhh..." Beautiee started sucking harder and Bazil grabbed her head and fucked her mouth as his legs trembled... "Uuuggghhhh..... Uuuggghhhh... Uuuggghhh!" Beautiee swallowed and continued sucking for a few moments until Bazil stopped her... "Beautiee..."

"Yes... My Thirst Quencher..."

"I need a minute..." Bazil said as he stepped back and laid down next to Beautiee. Beautiee got up, got down between Bazil's legs, and slid down ... "Beautiee..." Bazil whispered...

"Yes... My Thirst Quencher..." Beautiee breathed as she took Bazil's dick in her mouth again...

"I... need... zzzzz...." Beautiee continued to suck his dick for a few moments and then she laid her head on his pelvis and went to sleep with him.

Chapter 10

"Starr... we need to talk..." Chandler said as he closed the door...

"Are you upset with me?"

"Sit down Starr..."

"Okay... I'm sorry..."

"You don't need to apologize... you just need to listen..."

"Okay..."

"I don't want you to let your mother go to the shelter..."

"You don't? Why?"

"Because we're getting married..."

"Chandler..." I whispered as I started crying...

"You told me you wanted to be happy... right?"

"Yes..." I sniffed...

"I know if your mother winds up in the shelter you won't be happy..." Chandler said as he handed me tissues...

"I won't be happy... but I was hoping if she went to the shelter it would change her mind and she would agree to pay my father rent – especially since he said it was okay for her to stay there..."

"See – this is what I'm talking about – you're stuck in the middle between your mother and your father – the only thing you should be focused on is our wedding..."

"I don't know what else to do Chandler..."

"Let your mother come stay here... with us..."

"No..."

"Starr..."

"No Chandler – I've waited a long time for you – I prayed for you – and now we're getting married – I want you all to myself – I want to enjoy being your wife – I want to enjoy my husband – love my husband – and I don't want my mother anywhere near that!"

"Okay then – I have another suggestion..."

"Okay..."

"Let your mother stay in your apartment..."

"I'll get evicted..."

"They have to give you 30 days – you'll be married and living with your husband by then..."

"What about my mother?"

"I'll talk to her..."

"What if she doesn't listen to you?"

"Really Starr? That's what you think of me?"

"I'm sorry Chandler..."

"Stop apologizing..." he said as he pulled me into a kiss...

"Okay..."

"Here's what you're gonna do..." he said as we continued kissing... "You're going to go to work tomorrow..."

"Okay..."

"You're going to request time off so we can get married..."

"Okay..."

"We're going to go on our honeymoon..."

"Okay..."

"You're going to see Ms. Cox on Friday..."

"Okay..."

"You're going to tell her you don't need your Section 8 anymore..."

"Okay..."

"You're going to let your mother stay in the apartment..."

"Okay..."

"I'm going to talk to your mother..."

"Okay..."

"And I'm going to talk to your father..."

"But..."

"I said... I'm going to talk to your father... understand?"

"Yes Chandler..."

"Now..." he said as we continued kissing... "You're going to tell me everything..."

"Okay..."

"And then... I'm going to make love to you..."

"Okay..."

"Now..." he said as he took my hands... "Give me all the details..." I got up, went to get my lap top, sat back down, and turned it on. I logged into my email and showed Chandler all the details for the wedding...

"This looks really romantic..."

"It does..."

"I can't believe they do all the planning for you..."

"I'm glad they do..."

"Beautiee did the damn thing..."

"She sure did..."

"Show me the honeymoon..."

"Okay..." I said as I clicked on it...

"Oh wow..."

"I was going to ask you... but Beautiee said I should surprise you..."

"I'm surprised..."

"Do you like it?"

"I love it..."

"Really?"

"Yes Starr... really..." he said as he kissed me...

"I love you..."

"I love you too..."

"Beautiee says we need passports..."

"I have one..."

"Beautiee says I need to make an appointment at the Connecticut Passport Agency in Stamford..."

"Okay... you'll make an appointment for Friday, May 31st."

"Okay..."

"What's happening Saturday?"

"Beautiee says we're going shopping for dresses..."

"Okay – I'll talk to your father... we need to go shopping too..."

"Okay..."

"Now... come with me..." Chandler said as he stood up...

"No..."

"Did you just tell me no?"

"Yes..."

"Why?"

"Because..." I said as I stood up, kissed him, and took his hand... "I want you to come with me..." I said as I walked him outside on the patio..."

"Starr..."

"Ssshhh..." I whispered as I pushed him away from me and started undressing him...

"Okay..." Chandler said, smiling. Chandler stood still and let me undress him completely, enjoying my hands on his chest, his back, his ass, and his dick. I stepped back, stood still, and closed my eyes. Chandler stepped closer to me, kissed me, and undressed me. I kept my eyes closed as he massaged my breasts, and I didn't open them until he told me to...

"Open your eyes..." he said as he grabbed my ass, pulled me close to him, and held my naked body against his. Chandler started kissing me, I opened my mouth so he could put his tongue inside, and we stood there holding each other, tonguing each other down. Chandler walked me backwards towards the lounger and pushed me down on it. It was cold so it shocked me at first, but Chandler got on top of me right away and started tonguing me down again before I could react. My legs were already open so he had no trouble easing himself inside me...

"Mmmm....." I moaned as he started thrusting. I was so turned on by the fact that we were outside on the deck and I loved feeling the cool breeze on my legs as Chandler continued thrusting...

"Mmmph! Mmmph! Mmmph..."

"Mmmm.... Mmmm..... Mmmm....." I heard the neighbors come out on their deck and start whispering...

"Honey... I think they're fucking..."

"Really?"

"Ssshhh... listen..."

"Mmmph! Mmmph! Mmmph..." I knew they were listening and it turned me on... "Mmmm.... Mmmm..... Mmmm....."

"Yea... they're fuckin'... "

"Let's join them..." I heard her say...

"You sure?" he asked...

"Hell yea – this shit's turning me on..." I heard her say...

"Yesss..." I heard him say...

"Mmmph! Mmmph! Mmmph..." Oh shit... fuck me..." I heard her say... and Chandler stopped kissing me to turn his head...

"Damn... you're so fuckin' wet... you're really turned on – aren't you?"

"Ohhh... yes..." she moaned. Chandler continued thrusting as he looked at me... and then we went back to tonguing each other down...

"Mmmph! Mmmph! Mmmph..."

"Damn... he's gettin' it in!" he said as he fucked his wife...

"Mmmm.... Mmmm..... Mmmm....." I moaned...

"Oh shit... Fuck me... I wanna come with them..." she moaned...

"Like this?" he gritted as he started fucking her harder. Not to be out done, Chandler started fucking me harder too...

"Chandler... Chandler... Chandler..."

"Charles... Charles... Charles..."

"Mmmph! Mmmph! Mmmph..."

"Shit... Fuck... Theresa... I'm cumming..."

"Chandler... Chandler... Chandler... Aaaahhhh!"

"Charles... Ohhh... Shit... Aaaaahhhh!"

"Mmmph! Mmmph! Mmmph! Mmmmmpppphhhhh!"

"Uuugghh!   Uuugghh!   Uuugghh!" Chandler and I continued tonguing each other down as we listened to them...

"Shit – I need to thank my new neighbors – that was so fuckin' intense..." she said...

"Fuck yea..." he said...

"We should've done this a long time ago..." she said...

"I can't wait to do it again..." he said...

"I'ma knock on their glass to let'em know were outside so they can fuck too..." she said...

"You think they'll be open to it?' he asked...

"I hope so – that shit turned me on..."

"Are you?" Chandler asked...

"Yes..." I breathed...

"So am I..."

Chapter 11

"Good morning..." our neighbors said as we closed the door...

"Good morning Charles... Good morning Theresa..." Chandler said.

"Good morning Chandler..." Theresa said. "What's your name Sweetie?" she asked me...

"Hi Theresa... I'm Starr..."

"It's lovely to meet you!" Theresa beamed...

"It's nice meeting you too..." I said. Chandler and Charles looked at us, looked at each other, and fist-bumped...

"Thank you for last night..." Theresa said...

"Yes... thank you..." Charles said...

"You're welcome... I guess..." I laughed...

"To be honest — we've been out of touch lately... until last night..." Theresa said...

"And we've been touching each other ever since..." Charles said as he kissed her...

"I didn't think you were home..." I said...

"Oh my God – you didn't mean for us to hear you?" Theresa asked...

"Not really..."

"Oh my God – I'm so sorry..." Theresa said...

"You don't have to apologize... I liked it..." I said. Chandler and Charles looked at each other and smiled...

"You did?"

"Yea... we did..." I said as I put my arm around Chandler and pulled him close to me...

"Maybe we can get together sometime..." Charles said...

"We'll meet you out on the terrace again..." Chandler said...

"Oh good – summer's coming – we'll be out on our patio just about every night..." Theresa said...

"I'll be out there a lot more now that I'm getting married..." Chandler said...

"You're engaged? Congratulations!" Charles said...

"Thank you..."

"I see you're off to work – have a good day Sergeant..." Charles said...

'Call me Chandler..."

"Okay – Chandler..."

"You both have a good day too – let's go Starr..."

"Okay — bye Theresa - bye Charles..." I said as we got in the elevator... "They seem really nice..."

"They are..."

"You okay Chandler?"

"I'm fine Starr — I just like to keep my guard up..."

"What do you mean?"

"The first thing he does is call me Sergeant — I don't do favors for people — and I don't need anybody calling me Sergeant outside of work..."

"Okay..."

"I didn't really go on my patio until you and I started seeing each other..."

"Ohh... I'm sorry..."

"I told you before..." he said as he pulled me into a kiss... "Stop apologizing..."

"It's just that I was so happy... and I was in a mood..."

"I know..." he said as he kissed me again... "And I love it!"

"I was really turned on..."

"I know..."

"And it felt so good..."

"It did..."

"It turned me on when they caught us..."

"I know it did..."

"So... it's okay if we do it again?"

"Starr?"

"Yes Chandler?"

We can do it anywhere you want..." he said as he kissed me... "Anytime you want..." he said as he kissed me again... "As much as you want..."

"Mmmm... okay..."

"We can stop this elevator..." he said as he started kissing my neck... "And we can do it right now... right here..."

"Oh Chandler..." I breathed... "I need to go to work..."

"You want me... don't you?"

"Yes..."

"Come with me..." he said as we went down to the first floor...

"Good morning Mr. Chandler – Good morning Mrs. Chandler..." the doorman said when he saw us...

"Good morning..." we both said in unison. When we got outside I waited for Chandler to open the door for me but he opened the back door instead...

"Get in..."

"In the back seat?" Chandler folded his arms and waited... "Okay..." I said as I got in and Chandler got in beside me... "Chandler..."

"Lay down..." I did as I was told. Chandler laid down on top of me and started kissing me...

"Chandler... we'll get caught..."

"No we won't..."

"You sure?"

"Trust me..." he said as he unbuttoned my pants, unzipped them, and pulled them down to my ankles. I kicked my foot out my pants so I could open my legs. Chandler loosened his holster, loosened his pants, and pulled them down enough so he could free his dick and ease it inside me...

"Chandler..." I moaned...

"Ssshhhh..." he breathed in my neck...

"I can't help it..." I breathed. Chandler covered my mouth with his and started fucking me hard... "Mmmmm! Mmmmm! Mmmmm! Mmmmm!"

"Mmmph! Mmmph! Mmmph! Mmmph!"

Mmmmm! Mmmmm! Mmmmm! Mmmmm!"

"Mmmph! Mmmph! Mmmph! Mmmph!"

"Oohhh...Chandler... I'm cumming!"

"Mmmph! Mmmph! Mmmph! Mmmph!" Chandler lay on top of me, kissing me until our orgasms subsided and then he got up and fixed his clothes... "Get dressed – I'll take you to work..."

"Okay..." I said as I got dressed and adjusted myself. After Chandler made sure we were both okay he opened the back door, we both got out, and then Chandler opened the door so I could get in the front seat. Once I got in, Chandler closed the door then he got in himself...

"How do you feel?"

"Wonderful..." I sighed. Chandler smiled as he started the car...

"I'ma swing by dunkin donuts before I take you to work – okay?"

"Yes Chandler..." I sighed...

"You alright?" he asked as he took my hand...

"Yea..." I sighed...

"Wanna do it again?"

"Yes Chandler..."

"Okay..." he said as he pulled up to dunkin donuts...

"May I take your order?" the cashier asked...

"Yea – I want one extra-large coffee – hazelnut – hazelnut swirl –light with cream – you want one Starr?"

"Yea..."

"Make that two – and two Big N Toasty..."

"Okay – please pay at the window..." the cashier said as Chandler drove up to the window, paid, and waited. When he got the food and coffee, he found a spot and parked the car...

"Starr..."

"Yes Chandler?"

"You okay?"

"Yes..." I sighed...

"We're gonna eat breakfast here so I can spend some more time with you before I go to work..."

"Okay..." I said as I started eating...

"Talk to me..."

"I'm getting nervous..." I said as I took another bite...

"So am I..." Chandler said as he took a bite...

"Really?"

"Yea..."

"We're getting married..."

"I know..."

"There's so much to do..."

"I know..."

"I'm so happy Chandler..."

"I'm happy too..."

"I hope Ms. Hurley understands..."

"Why wouldn't she?"

"I just started the job..."

"Don't worry about that..."

"Okay..."

"I'ma talk to your parents today..."

"I know..."

"Don't worry about either..."

"I can't help it Chandler..."

"Starr..." he said as he took my hand...

"Yes Chandler?"

"Everything's going to be okay... I promise..." he said as he started the car. I didn't say anything. I just drank my coffee and looked out the window as he drove to New Haven. "Starr..."

"Yes Chandler?" Chandler kissed me. When I tried to get out, he pulled me back into another kiss... "Chandler... I..."

"I know..." he said and then he kissed me again...

"I love you so much..."

"I love you too..."

"I gotta go – I can't be late for work..." I laughed...

"Tell 'em you're under arrest..." Chandler laughed...

"I'll call you..." I said as I got out and started walking towards admissions...

"Hey Starr – was that your father?" one of the students asked me...

"That wasn't my father – that was my husband..." I answered as I went inside...

"Well good morning! I see you made it back!" Ms. Hurley said when she saw me...

"Yea..." I sighed...

"Oh no – what happened?"

"A lot..." I sighed...

"Are you quitting?"

"No..."

"You sure?"

"Yea..."

"Is everything alright?" I couldn't hold it in any more – I burst into tears...

"Oh my God – Starr – what happened?"

"This happened!" I yelled and showed her my hand...

"Oh my God! You're getting married! Congratulations!" she said as she pulled me into a hug…

"Thank you…"

"Who's the lucky man?"

"Sergeant Chandler…"

"Sergeant Chandler? From Bridgeport?"

"Yes…"

"Oh wow… he's a good man…"

"You know him?"

"My son is a Sergeant at the precinct in Fairfield – he talks about Chandler all the time…"

"Aww… wait 'till I tell Chandler…"

"So have you set a date?"

"I wanted to talk to you about that…"

"Tell me…"

"We're getting married on Thursday, June 6th…"

"Okay – that's two weeks from today…"

"and our cruise to Bermuda leaves on Friday, June 7th – and returns on Friday, June 14th…"

"So – basically – you'll be here a couple of days – then you'll be gone a week – then you'll be back – tell ya what – since you don't get back from your cruise until Friday, June 14th – you don't have to come in that Saturday…"

"Thank you Ms. Hurley!"

"Call me Amy…"

"Thank you Amy…"

"You're welcome – now – we better get to work – you're only gonna be here a couple of days..." she laughed...

"Good morning Chandler..." Bazil answered...

"I need to see you at Thelma's today at 12 pm for lunch..."

"Okay... I'll be there..."

"I'm also inviting Mary – just to give you a heads-up..."

"Thank you – I appreciate that..." Bazil said as he hung up...

"Good morning Chandler..." Mary answered...

"I need you to meet me at Thelmas at 12 pm for lunch today...

"Oh wow – I'll be there – thanks for inviting me to lunch..."

"You're welcome – I'll see you this afternoon..." Chandler said as he hung up... "Now let's see..." he said as he looked on line and did a search for apartment leases... "This one looks good..." he said as he printed it out... "Now I'll just fill this out and bring it with me – Thompson?"

"Yea Sarge?"

"I'ma run to the bank real quick – I'll be right back..." Chandler said as he went to his car...

"Okay Sarge..." Thompson said as Chandler drove off...

"Mr. Chandler – how can we help you today?" the teller asked...

"I need a cashier's check for $5,000.00..."

"You'll need to see the Manager..."

"No problem..."

"Mr. Chandler –how are you?" Marlowe asked when he saw him...

"I'm good, I'm good..."

"What can we do for you today?"

"I'm waiting to see the Manager..."

"He'll be right with you – if there's anything I can do – please let me know...

"Mr. Chandler – please come to my office..." the Manager said...

"Okay..." Chandler said as he followed the Manager into his office and sat down...

"I understand you need a cashier's check for $5,000.00..."

"That's right..."

"I'll be right back – it'll be just a few minutes..." the Manager said as he got up and went to get the check... "Here ya go Mr. Chandler..." the Manager said as he handed the check to Chandler..."

"Thank you..."

"Have a good day..."

"You too..." Chandler said as he headed back to work..."

"Chandler!" Charles said when he saw him...

"Hey Charles..."

"Listen – I know you're at work – I don't wanna keep you – but I gotta tell you something..."

"What's that?"

"I wanted to thank you..."

"For what?"

"You saved my marriage..."

"Really?"

"My wife stopped wanting me a long time ago... until last night..." he said as he smiled...

"I'm happy for you..."

"I don't know what happened – but when she heard you and Starr... something happened...

"We heard..." Chandler said as they both laughed...

"I'ma let you go Chandler – I'll see you on the terrace!" Charles yelled as he went on his way and Chandler went back to the precinct. Chandler spent the rest of the morning catching up on reports, stats, etc...

"Shit – it's just about 12 – le'me get over to Thelmas..." he said as he got up to leave... "Guys – I'm at lunch – I'll be back..." Chandler said as he headed to Thelmas. When he got there, Bazil was already seated. Chandler went to sit at the table with him...

"You're back – did you ask this gentleman to come make me smile?" the waitress asked...

"Naa... he's taken — but if you're interested, I can bring someone here to meet you..."

"What can I get you to drink?"

"A pitcher of sweet tea — and another setting – they'll be three of us..."

"Is that pretty lady joining you?"

"Not today..."

"Okay – I'll be right back..."

"What was that all about?" Bazil asked...

"I was here yesterday with Starr and she asked me if I had any brothers because she wants a man to make her smile..."

"Oh... I see..."

"Le'me give this to you before Mary get's here..." Chandler said as he handed Bazil the cashiers check...

"What's this for?"

"The honeymoon..."

"Okay..." Bazil said as he put the check away and Mary walked in...

"What's he doing here?" Mary snapped as she sat down...

"Hello Mary..." Bazil said...

"May I take your orders?" the waitress asked...

"Smothered pork chops for me..." Chandler said...

"Same sides?"

"Yes..."

"How 'bout you Maam?"

"Party wings, mac & cheese, collard greens…"

"And you sir?"

"Party wings, mac & cheese, collard greens…"

"Okay! I'll be back shortly…" the waitress said as she walked away…

"I need to talk… and you both need to listen…"

"Okay Chandler…" Bazil said…

"Mary?"

"Alright, alright…"

"Starr is going to be my wife…"

"Okay…" Bazil and Mary said in unison…

"and she's not happy…"

"Here we go…" Mary said…

"Respectfully – I'm not done talking…"

"Sorry Chandler – go ahead…"

"She's not happy – and I'm not either…"

"Why aren't you happy Chandler?" Bazil asked, even though he already knew the answer…

"I'm not happy because my wife is caught in the middle between the two of you and your shit!" Chandler snapped…

"Wait a minute Chandler…"

"Mary – let me stop you right there…" Chandler said…

"Let the man speak Mary…"

"Who the fuck do you think you're talking to Bazil?"

"See – this – this shit right here – this is what the fuck I'm talkin' about – le'me tell you both something – if either of you upsets my wife on her wedding day – it's gonna be a fuckin' problem · and neither of you will see Starr again..."

"With all due respect Chandler – you can't stop me from seeing my daughter..."

"With all due respect... try me... if you want to..."

"Okay Chandler – you're right – Starr shouldn't be in the middle of this..."

"Did you even think about your daughter when you delivered your message to me yesterday?" Mary asked...

"I thought about her as much as you did when you called to deliver your message to me..." Bazil answered...

"Here's what's gonna happen..." Chandler interrupted. Bazil and Mary stopped to look at Chandler... "Mary – you're not going to the shelter..."

"I'm not?"

"No – you're going to stay in the apartment..."

"Starr will get evicted..."

"Starr won't be homeless – she'll be with her husband..."

"Where does that leave me?" Mary asked...

"I'm glad you asked..." Chandler said as he pulled out the lease he printed...

"What the hell is this?" Mary snapped...

"Bazil made you an offer – and you're going to take it..." Chandler said as he put the lease in front of Mary to read...

"I'm not signing this shit!" Mary snapped...

"Yes you are..." Chandler said...

"What if I don't?"

"Starr's meeting with Ms. Cox on Friday..."

"So what?"

"So... she's going to tell Ms. Cox she doesn't need her Section 8 anymore... so the rent is only paid until the end of May... you don't really have a choice... well – actually – the shelter is a choice – I guess – but don't count on Starr dropping by the shelter too often..." Bazil sat there smiling, drinking his sweet tea. Mary was seething... and Bazil was enjoying every minute of it...

"Gimmie a damn pen!" Mary mumbled..."

"Here ya go..." Chandler said as he handed Mary a pen...

"There!" Mary snapped... "I signed it – are you happy Bazil?"

"Starr will be happy – that's what matters..." Bazil answered...

"Here ya go Bazil..." Chandler said as he handed Bazil the pen...

"What's this for?"

"Your signature is required here..." Chandler said as he pointed to where Bazil needed to sign...

"Done..." Bazil said...

"Good – I'll get Starr's signature on this lease – Mary – I'll make sure you get a copy to bring down to Social Services so you can apply for rental assistance..."

"Here's your food..." the waitress said as she put the food on the table...

"I'll take mine to go..." Mary said as she got up to leave..."

"I'll get it wrapped for you..." The waitress said as she took Mary's food back into the kitchen...

"Thank you Chandler..." Bazil said...

"You're welcome..."

"You know you couldn't ever stop me from seeing my daughter right?" Bazil laughed...

"Probably not... but I'm glad you didn't try me..." Chandler laughed as they ate...

"I'll fix his mutha-fuckin' ass – Starr probably put Chandler up to this shit – that's okay though – I got something for all their asses – Bazil – Chandler – and Starr – she thinks she can just forget me – after all I've done for her – okay – watch this..." Mary said as she dialed the number...

"Thank you for calling Attorney Smalls – this is Valarie – how may I help you?"

"I need an appointment for a consultation..."

"What's the issue?"

"Child support – do you handle child support cases?"

"Yes – we take child support cases – may I have your name?"

"Mary Smith…"

"May I have the name of the child?"

"Starr Osgood…"

"Father's name?"

"Bazil Osgood…"

"How many weeks does he owe you?"

"He owes me years in child support…"

"How many years?"

"Twenty Two…"

"Are you telling me Bazil BeBlanc never paid child support?"

"That's what I'm telling you…"

"Okay – may I have your number?"

"203-508-2798."

"Okay Ms. Smith – I'll give this message to Attorney Smalls – and he'll get back to you…"

"Thank you Valarie…"

"He's not gonna like this…" Valarie said as she called Smalls over the intercom…

"Yes Valarie?"

"I have a consultation for you…"

"Okay – bring it in…"

"You're not going to like this…" Valarie said…

"Show me…"

"Okay…" Valarie sighed as she handed Smalls the message and he started reading…

"Oh shit!"

"See?"

"Valarie – call her back – tell her I can see her tomorrow...

"Isn't that a conflict of interest?"

"Yes it is..."

"Oh... I get it – you're gonna pump her for information – then tell your client what she's up to..." Smalls didn't answer Valarie – he just smiled....

"Hello Ms. Smith – this is Valarie from Attorney Smalls office..."

"Wow – that was fast..."

"Mr. Smalls can see you tomorrow..."

"What time?"

"What time is good for you?"

"I need to take the bus – how 'bout 10:00?"

"Okay –see you tomorrow at 10 a.m."

"Hey Chan..." I sighed. Chandler pulled me into a kiss and held me... "Mmmm.... I love it when you kiss me like that..." Chandler kissed me again. I opened my mouth and we stood in the foyer, tonguing each other down for about 5 minutes...

"I have something to show you..." Chandler said as he took me into the kitchen and sat me in the chair at the island. I watched Chandler go into the refrigerator, take out a bottle of champagne, take down two glasses, pop the bottle, and pour us champagne...

"What are we celebrating?" I asked as he put a glass of champagne in front of me...

"See for yourself..." Chandler answered as he slid the envelope in front of me. I took the envelope, took out the lease, and read it...

"Chandler..." I whispered as I cried... is this for real?"

"It's for real Starr..." he said as he handed me a pen... "What's this for?"

"You need to sign it right there..." he said as he pointed to the line for my signature..."

"Okay..." I cried as I signed the lease and put down the pen...

"Now..." Chandler said as he put the lease back in the envelope... "I'm going to make sure your father gets this... "He said as he kissed me... "Your father will make sure Mary gets a copy..." he said as he kissed me again..." and we're going to celebrate..." he said as he picked up the glass of champagne. I picked up my glass of champagne and Chandler said, "Here's to happiness from now on..."

"To happiness from now on..." I cried...

"Drink your champagne Starr..." Chandler said as he drank his glass in a few gulps...

"Woa..." I laughed as I finished my glass... "I'm feeling tipsy..."

"Put your arms around my neck..."

"Okay..." I giggled as Chandler picked me up in his arms and carried me into the bedroom...

"Beautiee – where are you?" Bazil called out as he came in...

"I'm upstairs..."

"Meet me in the kitchen..."

"Okay – I'll be right there..." Beautiee said as she came downstairs and went into the kitchen...

"Oh wow! Bazil!" Bazil went over to Beautiee, held her, and kissed her deeply... "This is beautiful..." Beautiee cried as she looked around the kitchen. Bazil decorated the kitchen with trays of assorted fruits, cheese, meats, roses, balloons, and bottle of sparkling cider...

"This is for you..." Bazil said as he pulled her into a kiss again...

"I don't know what I did... but I'm glad I did it..." she breathed...

"I love you so much..."

"I love you too..." Beautiee whispered...

"Come sit down..." Bazil said as they sat at the table and he took her hands... "Ever since you found out I had a daughter you embraced her, and now you love her..."

"Of course..."

"You've comforted her, you've consoled her, you went to bat for her – with me – you convinced me that it was in her best interest to help her so she could help her mother – and now – you're helping her plan her wedding, you're making sure her mother is included – and now..." he said as he kissed her... "We're going to celebrate..."

"What are we celebrating?"

"I had lunch with Chandler today..." he said as he got up from the table and started making plates... "and Mary..."

"You did?'

"I did..." Bazil said as he put the plates on the table and went to pour the sparkling cider...

"How'd that go?'

"It was actually entertaining..." Bazil laughed...

"How?"

"Chandler basically told us he was tired of his wife being in the middle of our shit..." Bazil laughed...

"Oh I know this is gonna be good..." Beautiee laughed as Bazil sat at the table with two glasses of sparkling cider...

"It gets better..." Bazil laughed...

"Tell me..."

"He said..." he laughed... "If his wife was upset on her wedding day it was going to be a fuckin' problem – and here's the best part..."

"What?"

"He said he'd make sure we don't see Starr ever again! Ahhhaaaa! Ahhhaaaaa!"

"Oh shit!" Beautiee laughed... "What'd you say?"

"I told him he couldn't stop us from seeing Starr – and he said try me! Ahhhhaaaaa! Ahhhaaaaa!"

"Stop... my stomach..." Beautiee laughed...

"I have to admit – I loved that he was willing to stand up to us for Starr – but that's not the best part…"

"What happened?"

"Let's eat…"

"Okay – but you're gonna tell me right?"

"Of course…" Bazil said as he started eating and drinking…" Chandler told Mary Starr was going to tell Ms. Cox that she didn't need her Section 8 anymore – and the rent was only paid until the end of May – she didn't really have a choice but to sign the lease – unless she chose to go to the shelter – but she better not expect Starr to come visit…"

"Oh my God!" Beautiee said as she started eating and drinking…

"Beautiee…"

"What?!"

"Mary signed the lease…"

"Oh Bazil!"

"Chandler brought the lease with him – he had Mary sign it first – and then he had me sign it – Starr's signing it right now…"

"Oh thank God!"

"You're welcome…" God said…

"Mary was so mad she took her food to go – and left! Aaahhhaaaa! Aaaahhhaaaa!"

"So you and Chandler finished lunch?"

"Yes Beautiee…" Bazil said as he handed Beautiee the cashier's check…

"What's this for?"

"Chandler's reimbursing us for the honeymoon..." Bazil said as they finished eating.

Chapter 12

"Good morning Sheddi..." Bazil answered...

"Good morning Mr. Osgood – I'm calling with an update on the property you purchased..."

"Okay..."

"We're all set – we can close as soon as tomorrow if you like..."

"What time?"

"I can meet you at your attorney's office at 10 a.m."

"I'll call my attorney and get right back to you..." Bazil said as he hung up and called Smalls...

"Hey Bazil – I was just getting ready to call you – we need to talk..."

"I know..."

"You know?"

"Yea – Sheddi just called me – she said we can meet at your office tomorrow at 10 a.m."

"That won't work for me – see if we can meet her at her office at 12..."

"Okay..." Bazil said as he hung up and called Sheddi back...

"Hello Mr. Osgood..."

"Sheddi – my attorney can't do 10:00 – can we meet at your office at 12?"

"That's perfect – see you tomorrow at my office at 12..."

"Okay Sheddi..." Bazil said as he hung up...

"Hi Daddy..." I answered..."

"Starr – you can't go to work tomorrow..."

"Why Daddy?"

"We have an appointment tomorrow at 12:00 at Sheddi's office..."

"I get my keys?"

"Yes Starr – you get your keys..."

"Okay – I'll go tell Amy..."

"Who's Amy?"

"My supervisor..."

"Okay – see you tomorrow..."

"It's official Beautiee..."

"What?"

"Starr gets her keys tomorrow..."

"Bazil... that's wonderful..."

"C'mere..." Bazil said as he pulled Beautiee into a kiss...

"Mmmm... good morning to you too..."

"It's all because of you..." he said as he kissed her again...

"Naa..."

"What makes you say that?"

"You would've done something eventually..."

"You're right..." he said as he kissed her again... "but you..."

"We..."

"Cant argue with that..."

"Now Starr can get married... and be as happy as we are..."

"Naa..."

"What makes you say that?"

"We've had more practice..." he said as he pulled Beautiee down onto her back, put her arms above her head, got on top of her, opened her legs, eased himself inside her, and began kissing her while simultaneously thrusting...

"Hey Starr..."

"Chandler..."

"Yes Starr..."

"Chandler..." I cried...

"What's wrong?"

"I... I..."

"I'm on my way..."

"Wait..."

"What's going on?"

"Im happy..." I cried...

"Okay! That's better!" Chandler said as he smiled...

"I get my keys tomorrow..."

"Aww..."

"My mother doesn't have to go to the shelter..."

"No ... she doesn't..."

"I'll be able to see my mother every day..."

"Yes you will..."

"I love you Chandler..."

"I love you too..."

"We're getting married..."

"Yes we are..."

"I gotta get back to work..."

"Oh my God – you must be talking to Chandler..." Amy said as she came over to my desk...

"Yes... I am..."

"Tell him I said hello..."

"Amy says hello Chandler..."

"Amy? Amy Hurley?"

"Yea..."

"Amy's your supervisor?"

"Yea..."

"I went to the academy with her son..."

"I know – she told me yesterday..."

"She did? Why didn't you tell me?"

"We were busy celebrating..."

"True dat..."

"I gotta go Chandler..."

"Okay – see you tonight..."

"See you tonight... I need to tell you something Amy..."

"You need to leave – its fine – go ahead..."

"No Amy – I can stay..."

"Oh thank God..."

"You're welcome..." God said...

"I can't come in tomorrow though..."

"Can you come in Saturday?"

"Yes..."

"Okay – that's fine..."

"Come in Ms. Smith..." Smalls said as he invited Mary into his office... "Have a seat..."

"Thank you..." Mary said...

"Now – I understand you want to sue Bazil Osgood for back child support?"

"Damn right..."

"Did you ever have a DNA test done?"

"No..."

"But you're sure he's the father?"

"What the fuck are you trying to say?"

"Ms. Smith – please – I'm sorry if I offended you – I didn't mean to..."

"I'm sorry – I'm just so angry..."

"Why?"

"Because he never paid me any child support!"

"Why?"

"Ask him!"

"Ms. Smith... I'm not trying to make you uncomfortable – but I need to ask these questions..."

"I was with another man at the time – and he wanted children – so I let him believe my child was his..."

"Did Bazil know this?"

"Yea..."

"Did he sign the birth certificate?"

"Yea..."

"Okay... now I understand – but I need to ask you another question..."

"Okay..."

"Why did you wait 22 years to ask for child support?"

"Because he's charging me rent..."

"I don't understand..."

"He bought his daughter a co-op – but he won't let me stay in the co-op unless I pay him rent..."

"Ms. Smith – I have to be honest..."

"Okay..."

"This is coming across as petty..."

"Who the hell do you think you're talking to – you know what – fuck you!"

"I understand – I can refer you to another attorney..."

"Why would you do that?"

"Ms. Smith – regardless of how you feel about me – I'm an attorney first – you came in for a consultation – I have a reputation to maintain – having said that – I need to tell you something…"

"What?"

"Bazil Osgood is my client…"

"You son-of-a-bitch – you didn't give a damn about me – all you care about is Bazil…"

"Valarie?" Smalls asked as he called her on the intercom…

"Yes Smalls…"

"Please come into my office…"

"Yes Smalls?" Valarie said as she came into his office…

"Please give Conrad a call and put him through when you get him on the phone – and please give his information to Ms. Smith…"

"I don't want your fuckin' referral!" Mary snapped…

"Come with me Ms. Smith…" Valarie said. Mary followed her out of the office…

"I'm not taking the referral…"

"Ms. Smith – please reconsider…"

"Why? Why the fuck would I do that?"

"Because – Smalls only refers people if he believes they have a case…"

"Really? He thinks I have a case? How do you know that?"

"Trust me – if you didn't have a case – he would've told you that…"

"So – let me make sure I understand – he represents Bazil – I want to sue him – and he's referring me to another attorney – and he believes I have a case against his client?"

"Yes... that's right..."

"Bullshit! What's in it for him?"

"Smalls is an honorable, reputable attorney. He has a good reputation..."

"Okay – I'll take the referral..."

"Here..." Valarie said as she handed Mary the referral and Mary left. "Smalls?"

"Yes Valarie..."

"I have Conrad on the phone..."

"Smalls – how are you?"

"Not good..."

"Oh boy..."

"I'm referring Mary Smith to you..."

"Why?"

"She came to see me for a consultation..."

"Okay..."

"She's suing for back child support..."

"Okay – I love going after dead beat dads – who's the father?"

"Bazil Osgood..."

"Oh shit! Your client?"

"Yea..."

"Smalls?"

"Yea?"

"Does she have a case?"

"She'll be calling you later today..." Smalls said as he hung up...

"You okay?" Valarie asked as she came in...

"Hell no!" Smalls answered as he threw everything off his desk onto the floor...

"Conrad Cox speaking..."

"Mr. Cox – this is Mary Smith..."

"Hello Ms. Smith – I've been expecting your call..."

"Can you see me now?"

"Yes – I have some time available – come see me..."

"Okay – I'm on my way..."

"Dominique?"

"Yes Mr. Cox?"

"I have a Mary Smith coming to see me – I need you to prepare some papers..."

"Does she have an appointment?"

"No – why?"

"I'm meeting my husband for lunch at 12:00..."

"I'm sorry – I may need you to work past 12:00..."

"Can't I do the paperwork when I come back?"

"Tell you what – we'll see how it goes – she's not here yet – here's what I have so far – you can start the paperwork now and we'll see what happens when she gets here..."

"Okay Mr. Cox..."

"I can't wait to get to his office..." Mary said out loud as she got on the bus headed towards Trumbull. Mary sat down and looked out the window the entire way. "Good – I'm here..." she said as she got off the bus and headed to his office...

"How may I help you?" Dominique asked as Mary walked in...

"I'm here to see Mr. Cox..."

"May I tell him your name?"

"Mary Smith..."

"Hello Ms. Smith – he's expecting you – come with me..." Dominique said as Mary followed her into the office... "Mr. Cox, this is Mary Smith..."

"Thank you Dominique – Ms. Smith – have a seat..." Conrad said as Dominique closed the door and went back to her desk... "Ms. Smith – how can I help you?"

"I'm suing Bazil Osgood for back child support..."

"How old is the child?"

"Smalls didn't tell you?"

"Ms. Smith?"

"Yea?"

"Smalls represents Bazil Osgood – if I take your case – I'm representing you..."

"What the fuck you mean if?"

"Ms. Smith –let me be clear..." he sighed...

"Yea?"

"As your attorney – if I decide to take your case – you can't speak to me like that..."

"I'm sorry... but you said if..."

"I only take cases I can win – unless you have a healthy retainer..."

"Oh so if I can't pay you won't take my case?"

"That's not what I said – I said I only take cases I can win..."

"Oh so if I had money you'd take my case regardless..."

"Yes..."

"Well – Smalls thinks I have a case..."

"Ms. Smith – we're here to talk about you..."

"You're right – I'm sorry..."

"Now... how old is the child?"

"Twenty Two..."

"Bazil Osgood has a child with you that's twenty two years old – and he never paid child support?"

"No..."

"Why?"

"I was with another man at the time – he wanted children – so I let him believe my daughter was his..."

"Did Bazil sign the birth certificate?"

"Yes..."

"Did you ever have a DNA test done?"

"No..."

"Ms. Smith – is there a chance Bazil's not the father?"

"I don't think so..."

"Were you married to this other man?"

"No..."

"Why are you seeking child support now? After 22 years?"

"Because he bought my daughter a co-op – he made me sign a lease – and he expects me to pay him rent..." Conrad sat there shaking his head...

"Mr. Cox?"

"Yes Dominique?" Conrad said as he answered the intercom...

"My husband Sheldon is here to take me to lunch – is it okay if I go?"

"Sure – have the service take the calls – I'll see you when you get back – enjoy your lunch – and give my regards to Sheldon..."

"Thank you Mr. Cox – I will..." Domonique set the phones to go to the answering service and then she left with Sheldon...

"Ms. Smith – I'm not sure I can take this case..."

"Why not?"

"You've never had a DNA test done..."

"So what – can't the judge make him get a DNA test?"

"Ms. Smith?"

"What?"

"Bazil Osgood will tell the judge you said the child wasn't his..."

"He knew damn well Starr was his daughter..."

"The fact that you never had a DNA test done will look to the court like you knew it was possible the other man in your life was the father..."

"He owes me!"

"That may be true – but he can always argue that you never pursued it..."

"She had a father in her life!"

"Exactly!"

"What are you saying?"

"Your daughter's 22 years old..."

"So?"

"So she's over 21..."

"He still owes me!"

"Okay Ms. Smith – I'll take your case..."

"You will? Thank you, thank you, thank you! What do I do now?"

"I'll do the paperwork – and Bazil will get served..."

"Ha ha! Good!"

"That's all for now Ms. Smith – we'll be in touch..."

"Thank you..." Mary said as she danced out of Mr. Cox's office.

Chapter 13

"Good morning Starr..." Chandler said as he kissed me awake...

"Mmmm... good morning..."

"Are you ready to get up?"

"Yes... I'm ready to get up..." I said as I got up and straddled Chandler...

"Okay..." Chandler said as he grabbed my ass and eased himself inside me. I braced myself on Chandler's chest and started riding his dick...

"Uugghh... Uugghh... Uugghh..."

"Ooohhh... Ooohhh... Ooohhh..." Chandler pulled me down, held me, and kissed me as he kept thrusting...

"Uumph... Uumph... Uuumph..."

"Huu... Huu... Huu..." Chandler let go of me, moved his hands to my ass, and pushed me down on his dick and my clit started rubbing against his pelvis as he continued thrusting...

"Uuugghh... Uuugghh... Uuugghh..."

"Huu... Huu... Huu..."

"Fuck... I'm cumming..."

"I'm cumming with you..."

"Uuugh! Uuugh! Uuugh!

"Huu… Huu… Huu…"

"Uuuuuggghhhh!"

"Huuuuuhhhh!" I continued to lay there on top of Chandler as he held me and kissed me…

"I guess you were ready…" he said as we continued kissing…

"I was…"

"I can't wait for us to get married…"

"Neither can I…"

"Good luck today…"

"Thank you…"

"We'll celebrate again tonight when you get home…"

"Mmm…. Okay…"

"I have to get up now…"

"I don't want to…"

"I know…" Chandler said as he rolled me over and I pulled him back down on top of me…

"You know you in trouble now right?" he asked as he eased himself inside me and started thrusting…

"Yes Chandler…" I moaned…

"Good morning…" Bazil said as he kissed Beautiee awake…

"Mmmm…. Good morning…"

"How are you feeling?"

"Happy…"

"Come with me…" Bazil said as he helped Beautiee up off the bed and led her into the bathroom. He came into the bathroom, slid her nightgown off her shoulders, and let it drop to the floor...

"Bazil..."

"Ssshhh... stay there... I'll be right back..." he said as he went to get his phone. When he came back into the bathroom he walked up to Beautiee and kissed her...

"What are you doing?"

"Stay right there... just like that..." he said as he took her picture. Beautiee looked down, held her stomach, and Bazil took another picture... "You're beautiful..." he said as he put the phone down and pulled her into a kiss...

"Bazil..." she breathed as Bazil held her by the small of her back and continued kissing her. Bazil stepped away from her, undressed himself, and was standing in front of her completely nude. Beautiee smiled at him as he went into the shower and turned on the water. Bazil took her by the hand, led her into the shower, pulled her close to him, and kissed her deeply as the water beat down on them. Bazil started kissing her on her neck and she was enjoying it... "Oh Bazil... Bazil..."

"Yes... Beautiee..." he breathed as he began massaging her breasts. Beautiee threw her head back, closed her eyes, and let the water hit her face as Bazil began licking and sucking her breasts...

"Bazil... Bazil..." Bazil held her stomach and kissed her stomach all over and as he was doing so, Beautiee reached for Bazil's phone and took a picture of him kissing her stomach. Bazil took the phone from her, placed it by the sink, knelt down between her legs, and started flicking his tongue up and down on her clit... "Bazil!" she moaned as he put her leg up on his shoulder so he could put his tongue inside her... "Bazil... Bazil... Bazil..." she moaned as she grabbed his head and Bazil pushed her back against the shower wall as he continued licking and sucking... "Haaa.... Haaa.... Haaa..." she moaned as Bazil grabbed her ass in his hands and her legs began trembling... "Bazil! I'm cumming! Aaaahhhh!" Bazil put his tongue in her pussy and sucked on her juices as her orgasm subsided... and then he stood up, kissed her, and put his tongue in her mouth so she could taste herself. Bazil continued to tongue her down as he lifted her leg up, eased himself inside her, and began thrusting...

"Uumph! Uumph! Ummph!"

"Hhmph! Hhmph! Hhmph!"

"Uumph! Uumph! Ummph!"

"Hhmph! Hhmph! Hhmph!"

"Uumph! Uumph! Ummph!"

"Hhmph! Hhmph! Hhmph!"

"Uuuugggghhhh!" Bazil growled as he came but didn't stop thrusting...

"Hmmmmph! Hmmmmph! Hmmmmph!" Bazil slowed down a bit but continued thrusting until Beautiee's orgasm subsided...

"Are you still... happy?" he asked as he kissed her...

"Yeesss..." she breathed...

"Hi Daddy..." I said as soon as I saw him...

"Hi Starr..."

"Hey Bazil..." Smalls said as he walked up...

"Hey Smalls – this is my daughter – Starr..."

"Hi Starr – it's nice to meet you..." Smalls said as he took my hand and kissed it...

"It's nice to meet you too – you're my father's attorney?"

"I'm the family attorney..."

"Really?"

"Yes – I represent your father – I represent Beautiee – and today – I'm representing you..."

"Oh wow – I didn't even know I needed an attorney..."

"You always need an attorney for real estate transactions..."

"Ooohhh... Okay..."

"Bazil – we need to talk..."

"We'll talk inside when Sheddi gets here..."

"Bazil – I said we need to talk – now!"

"Starr – excuse us..." my father said as he walked a few feet away from me with Smalls...

"What's wrong?"

"Bazil – I'm sorry..." Smalls said as he served him ..."

"What the fuck is this?"

"Bazil – please – not here..."

"You should've thought of that before you served me this bullshit!" Bazil said as he ripped the paper in half and threw it back at Smalls..."

"Bazil..."

"Let's do this – we can talk later..."

"Is everything okay Daddy?"

"Yes Starr..." my father lied as he pulled me into a hug and kissed me on my forehead... "Everything's fine – let's go inside and get your keys..."

"Good morning everyone..." Sheddi said as she walked up to us...

"Good morning Sheddi – this is my daughter, Starr... and this is our attorney, Smalls..."

"Hello Starr – I'm your real estate agent..."

"Hi Sheddi – it's nice to meet you..."

"Hello Smalls – I represent the sellers as well as the buyers..."

"Hello Ms. Lemdon – it's nice to meet you..."

"Shall we all go inside?" Sheddi asked...

"Yes..."my father said as we all went inside...

"Good morning everyone – I'm Mr. Cox – I represent the seller…"

"Hi Mr. Cox – are you a real estate agent too?" I asked…

"He's an attorney Starr…" my father answered…

"Let's get started so my clients can get their keys…" Sheddi said…

"Okay – I understand both names are going on the title?"

"That's correct…" Smalls said…

"Here are the papers you both need to sign – if everything's in order, you both sign, and you get your keys…" Conrad said…

"Let me take a look at these…" Smalls said. I sat there and watched as Smalls took his time reviewing each sheet…

"Ms. Sheddi?"

"Yes Starr?"

"What happens next?"

"When your attorney is done reviewing the paperwork, you'll both sign the paperwork, and the title to the property will be sent to you as proof of ownership…"

"So I own a co-op with my dad?"

"Yes Starr…"

"I like that – thank you Daddy…"

"You're welcome Starr…"

"Everything is in order…" Smalls said as he pushed the papers in front of me…

"So I have to sign all of these?"

"Yes Starr..."

"Okay..." I said as I started looking them over. I saw the contract with the seller's information, the buyer's information, the attorneys, and Sharon Lemdon... "Who's Sharon?" I asked...

"I'm Sharon – but my friends call me Sheddi..." she said...

"Aww... I like that..." I said as I looked at the taxes, utilities, insurance, etc. When I was satisfied, I started signing the papers where indicated...

"Here Daddy..." I said as I pushed the papers in front of my father...

"I'll be done in a few minutes – and then... you can get your keys..." my father said as he signed the papers... Here ya go Conrad..." my father said as he pushed the papers in front of Mr. Cox...

"Thank you Mr. Osgood, Ms. Osgood – here's your keys – congratulations..."

"Thank you Daddy!" I said as I grabbed my father and hugged him tight...

"You're welcome – let's go see your new place..."

"Okay!"

"Thank you for everything Sheddi..." my father said...

"You're welcome Mr. Osgood – if you don't need anything else – I have another client waiting..."

"We're good – thank you again..." my father said...

"Bazil?"

"Yes Smalls?"

"I'm sorry..."

"I know..."

"Here..." he said as he put the torn paper in my father's pocket...

"C'mon Starr – let's go..." my father said as we got in the car...

"I'm so happy – I can't wait to see my new place..."

"I'm glad you're happy Starr..." We didn't talk after that. I watched my father as he drove. I knew something was on his mind but I also knew he wouldn't tell me...

"I can't wait until I get there..."

"I know..."

"Beautiee showed me pictures..."

"That's nice..."

"It's right near Chandler..."

"I know..."

"I'll be able to see my mother everyday..."

"I know..."

"Daddy – guess what?"

"What?"

"My supervisor knows Chandler..."

"She does?"

"Yes..."

"How?"

"Chandler went to the academy with her son – he's a sergeant in Fairfield..."

"Oh wow – that's nice..."

"She said her son talks about Chandler all the time..."

"That's really nice Starr..."

"Daddy – we're here!" As soon as my father parked the car I couldn't wait – I jumped out and ran up to the door... "C'mon Daddy – hurry up!"

"Okay..." my father laughed. I opened the door and went inside...

"Daddy! I love it! Thank you, thank you, thank you!" I yelled as I threw my arms around my father's neck and kissed him...

"You're welcome – why don't you give Chandler a call – I'm sure he'd like to see it..."

"Oh – that's a great idea!" I squealed as I called Chandler...

"Hey Starr..."

"Chandler – we're here!"

"Where?"

"Here! I got my keys!"

"You're at the new place?"

"Yes!"

"Text me the address – I'm on my way..."

"Daddy – I love you so much!"

"I love you too Starr..."

"Mommy doesn't have to go to the shelter... Chandler and I are getting married... you're having a baby... everybody's happy..."

"Yes we are Starr..."

"Starr – open the door..." Chandler said...

"Hi Chan..." I sighed as I opened the door, threw my arms around him, and gave him a big kiss...

"Hi Starr... you must be really happy – can I come in?"

"Oh – sorry..." I laughed as I let him in..."

"Oh wow – this is nice... your mother will really like it..."

"I know!"

"Where'd you get the furniture?"

"Daddy..."

"Bazil – you did this?"

"Yea..."

"Thank you – that was really sweet..."

"No need to thank me Chandler – Starr needed new furniture anyway..."

"This is right around the corner from me..."

"Yes it is..."

"You can see your mother every day..."

"Yes I can..."

"Bazil – I'll take Starr to see Ms. Cox..."

"Okay – I'll see you guys later..."

"Bye Daddy – I love you..." I said as I pulled him into a hug..."

"I love you too Starr – I'll see you soon..." my father said as he left...

"Hmmm... my dad seemed to be in a hurry..."

"C'mere…" Chandler said as he pulled me into a kiss…"

"Mmmm… that's nice…"

"So is that new bed in the bedroom…" Chandler said as he continued to kiss me while walking me backwards into the bedroom…

"Hi Ms. Crystal…" I said when I saw her…

"Hi Starr – come into my office…" I followed her inside and sat down… "Starr – I don't want you to get evicted – you worked too hard…"

"Ms. Crystal – I'm gonna be okay…"

"Starr – I know you have a job – but you haven't been there a week yet – are you sure you can afford the rent on your apartment without Section 8?"

"Ms. Crystal – I don't need my Section 8 anymore…"

"Starr – think about what you're doing…"

"I'm getting married!" I beamed as I showed her my ring…

"Oh wow – congratulations – when did you get engaged?"

"Remember when they told you I got out of a squad car?"

"Yea?"

"That's my husband…"

"You're engaged to a cop?"

"I'm engaged to Sergeant Chandler…"

"Hot Damn!" she said as she got up to give me a hug...

"And guess what else?"

"Tell me..."

"I have a co-op in downtown Bridgeport!" I yelled as I showed her my keys...

"How – ever mind – congratulations!"

"My father bought it for me!"

"Oh Starr – that's wonderful..."

"And guess what else?"

"What else girl?"

"My mother signed a lease! She's going to pay us rent – and the rent will cover the expenses!"

"Starr – how much is your mother's rent?"

"Less than $500 a month..."

"Oh wow! I'm so happy for you! Have you set a date?"

"Thursday, June 6th..."

"I love it when my clients have happy endings..."

"God answered all my prayers – and the answer was yes!"

"I'm so happy Starr..."

"Thank you..."

"So... you need to sign these papers stating that you're giving up your Section 8 at the end of this month..."

"Where do I sign?"

"Sign here... and here..." she said as she pointed to where I needed to sign...

"Thank you for everything Ms. Crystal..." I said as I hugged her...

"You're welcome – call me sometime – and I want a picture..."

"Okay – I gotta get going – bye!" I yelled as I headed over to Trumble Gardens...

"Hi Mommy!" I said out of breath when I got to the top of the stairs...

"Ms. Osgood... you're late..."

"What time is it?"

"It's 4"35..." the woman said...

"Five minutes – oh my goodness..."

"Ms. Osgood – this is a serious matter – you're in violation of your housing agreement and your Section 8..."

"I don't have Section 8 anymore..." I said as I sat down...

"I don't understand..."

"I just signed papers giving up my Section 8 Certificate..."

"Starr! Why in the hell would you do that?" my mother yelled...

"Because I don't need Section 8 anymore Mommy..."

"Ms. Osgood – we need to discuss..."

"I'm moving out – we won't be here in June..."

"We won't?" my mother asked...

"No Mommy – we won't – now Ms. – whatever your name is – please excuse us..." I said as I held the door open for her to leave...

"Fine –here's your eviction notice..." she said as she tried to hand it to me...

"I don't need it – we're moving out –have a nice day..." I laughed as I closed the door...

"Damn Starr – that was fucked up..." my mother laughed... "You didn't even get her name..."

"I don't care what her name is Mommy – we're outta here!" I yelled as I showed her my keys...

"You got the keys!"

"Yes Mommy! I got the keys!"

"Do we have to wait until the end of the month?"

"Nope..."

"Oh my God – I need to pack – we need to call the movers..."

"Mommy?"

"Yes Starr..."

"We don't need to call the movers..."

"Starr – how are we gonna get the furniture over to your new place?"

"We have new furniture..."

"We do?"

"Daddy bought it for me..."

"Aww... that's nice..." I noticed my mother's attitude change...

"You okay Mommy?"

"I'm okay Starr..." she sighed...

"C'mon Mommy – let's go see our new place!"

"Now?"

"Yes Mommy! I can't wait to show it to you!"

"Okay!" my mother said as we went downstairs to wait for the Uber. When we got there my mother was so excited... "Oh my God! Starr! It's beautiful!"

"Thank you Mommy!"

"I can't believe your father did all this..."

"I can..."

"You can?"

"Mommy – Daddy loves me..."

"Yes... he does..."

"Mommy?"

"Yes Starr?"

"You can take the #4 from Park Avenue and Jackson Avenue – or you can take the #3 from Madison Avenue and Thorme Street – or – you can walk – it's about a 30 minute walk though...

"Hmmm... I might walk... on a nice day..."

"Mommy – they have a coin-operated washer and dryer in the basement..."

"I don't have to go to the laundry mat?"

"Nope..."

"Can I stay here tonight?"

"Sure Mommy..."

"I wish we could move tomorrow..."

"We can't..."

"Why not?"

"Beautiee's taking us shopping for wedding dresses tomorrow..."

"Ohh... that's nice..."

"Mommy?"

"Yes Starr?"

"Are you sure you're okay?"

"I'm okay..."

"Mommy – Beautiee took care of everything..."

"She did?"

"Yes Mommy – and she said she needs your help because my lil' brother won't let her stand on her feet for too long..."

"What did Beautiee do?"

"Beautiee booked our wedding and our honeymoon..."

"Already? You set a date?"

"Yes Mommy – Thursday, June 6th..."

"When were you gonna tell me?"

"Here's the keys Mommy – I have the other set – I'm going to see Chandler – I'll see you tomorrow..." I said as I got up to leave...

"Starr!"

"Yes Mommy?"

"No hug?"

"Sorry Mommy..." I said as I hugged her...

"That's better..."

"Bye Mommy – be ready when I get off work tomorrow..." I said as I left...

"Good Lord... what the hell did I just do?" Mary sighed...

Chapter 14

"Bazil? Is that you?" Beautiee said as she came downstairs... "Bazil? Where are you? Hmmm... I guess it wasn't him..." she said as she went into the kitchen... "Bazil – you're home!" she said as she put her arms around him and started kissing his neck...

"Beautiee..."

"Yes... My Thirst Quencher..." she breathed...

"Stop it..." he said as he took her hands from around his neck and pushed her away from him...

"Bazil? What's wrong?" she asked with tears in her eyes...

"Beautiee... please... just leave me alone... okay?"

"Okay..." she whispered as she started crying. Beautiee went into the library and turned on the computer... "I'll do some writing... that'll make me feel better... shoot... there goes my phone... Hi Starr..."

"Hi Beautiee – what's wrong?"

"Nothing..."

"What's going on?"

"What do you mean Starr?"

"First Daddy, then Mommy... now you..."

"I don't understand..."

"We went to close today and I got my keys..."

"I know..."

"I was so happy but Daddy was somewhere else..."

"What do you mean?"

"Daddy was fine until Mr. Smalls got there – they were arguing – and then Daddy started acting funny..."

"Really?"

"I took my mother to the co-op and she was so happy – and then she started acting funny – and now you're acting funny..."

"I'm okay Starr – tell me about your mother..."

"Beautiee – she's so happy – she's at the co-op now – and guess what?"

"What Starr?"

"Daddy bought new furniture so I don't need anything!"

"Oh Starr – that's wonderful – I'm glad you're so happy..."

"It seems like me and Chandler are the only ones that are happy..."

"I'm happy too Starr..."

"No you're not... and neither is my father... and that's making me sad..."

"I know what will make you feel better..."

"What?"

"Take out your computer and go to David's Bridal.com..."

"Okay..."

"You see all the dresses they have?"

"Oh my God – they're all beautiful..."

"You pick out some you like – and I'll see you tomorrow when you get out of work..."

"Okay Beautiee... thank you..."

"You're welcome... see you tomorrow..."

"See you tomorrow Beautiee..."

"Hey Beautiee..." Smalls said as he answered the phone...

"What happened today?"

"He didn't tell you?"

"Would I be calling you if he did?"

"I gave him a letter..."

"What letter?"

"I have to go now – I'm getting another call..." Smalls said as he deliberately hung up...

"That's it – I'm getting to the bottom of this..." Beautiee said as she went into the kitchen to talk to Bazil... "Hmmm... he's not here – he must've gone upstairs – I'll bring him his jacket..." she said as she picked up the jacket and the torn letter fell out the pocket... "What the hell is this?" she asked out loud. Beautiee put the pieces of the torn letter together and read it...

"Oh my God..." she whispered. Beautiee went straight upstairs to the bedroom and saw Bazil sitting on their bed...

"Bazil..."

"Beautiee... please leave me alone..."

"No..." she said as she went closer to Bazil...

"Beautiee... please... leave me alone..." Beautiee didn't listen to him. She went over to him, stood in front of him, and pulled him to her. Bazil held Beautiee tight and started crying. Beautiee sat down on the bed next to him, held him, and let him cry on her shoulder...

Chapter 15

"Good morning..." Bazil answered...

"Good morning – did I wake you?" Chandler asked...

"Yea..."

"I was calling to tell you we're on our way..."

"Here?"

"Yes – Beautiee's taking Starr and Mary shopping for dresses today – remember?"

"Yea..."

"You sure you're okay Bazil?"

"Yea..."

"Okay – we're on our way..." he said as he hung up...

"Beautiee? Where are you?" Bazil asked as he got up... "Maybe she's downstairs..." he said as he went downstairs... "Beautiee – are you in the kitchen?"

"Yea..."

"Okay..." he said as he went into the kitchen...

"Hey Beautiful…" Bazil said as he tried to kiss her and she moved to the side to avoid it… "You made coffee?" he asked…

"Yea…"

"Thank you…" Beautiee didn't say anything – she just sat down and started drinking her coffee…"

"I'm sorry…" Beautiee didn't acknowledge his apology – she just finished her coffee… "Beautiee… please… I'm sorry…"

"So am I…" Beautiee said as she tried to go around Bazil and he grabbed her… "Let go of me Bazil…"

"No…"

"That's not what you said – or did – last night…"

"I was upset…"

"So what?"

"Smalls…"

"No Bazil – I don't wanna hear it…"

"Beautiee…"

"You pushed me away last night – you told me to leave you alone – and it hurt my feelings!"

"I'm sorry…" Bazil said as he started crying…

"I cried last night too – you didn't give a damn…"

"Beautiee… please… I'm sorry…" he said as he pulled her into a hug…

"Bazil – let go of me…"

"No…"

"Bazil… you're hurting me…"

"I'm sorry – I didn't know what to do…"

"How many fuckin' times do we have to go through something before you get it?"

"Get what?"

"All you had to do was talk to me – but you pushed me away…"

"You're right… I'm sorry…"

"You're sorry… and I'm tired…"

"You're tired? What's that supposed to mean?

"Just what I said…" Beautiee said as she went to get the door…

"Hi Starr – Hi Chandler…"

"Hi Beautiee – where's Bazil?"

"He's in the kitchen…" Beautiee said as she went into the living room and sat down…

"Beautiee – what's wrong?"

"I'm just tired Starr…"

"Are we still going to pick up Mommy?"

"I forgot – I'm sorry Starr…"

"I can go get her if you want…" Chandler said…

"No Chandler – that's okay – I'll go pick her up – I'll be back Starr – I need to get dressed…

"Can I come upstairs with you?"

"Sure – c'mon…" Beautiee said as I followed her upstairs…

"Beautiee?"

"Yes Starr?"

"Something's wrong... with you..."

"I know..."

"You wanna talk about it? I'm a good listener..."

"C'mere Starr..." Beautiee said...

"Yes Beautiee?"

"You're very sweet – I love you..." she said as she hugged me...

"I love you too... that's why I'm worried..."

"I'll be okay – le'me hurry up and get dressed so we can get your mother and go look at some dresses..."

"Okay..." I said as I looked around the room... "This room is so romantic..." I said as I sat on the bed... "I hope I'm this happy with Chandler..."

"Don't worry Starr – you will be..." my father said as he came into the bedroom...

"Beautiee's in the shower... Is she okay Daddy?"

"Yes Starr..."

"Are you okay?"

"I will be..."

"You still love Beautiee – right?"

"Starr..." Bazil said as he sat down on the bed next to her... "I will always love Beautiee..."

"You promise?"

"I promise..."

"Okay..."

"Oh... I see I have more company..." Beautiee said as she came out the shower...

"You want me to go downstairs?"

"Yes Starr – and take your father with you…"

"Okay – c'mon Daddy…" I said as I took my father's hand and pulled him out their room…

"Good – now I can get dressed in peace…" Beautiee said as she looked for something to wear.   After she got dressed, she came downstairs…

"You ready Beautiee?" I asked…

"Yes Starr – I'm ready…"

"Bye Daddy…" I said as I hugged him…

"Goodbye – see you later – Beautiee?"

"Yes Bazil?"

"I love you…" my father said as he pulled Beautiee into a kiss…

"I love you too – I'll see you later…" she said as she took my hand and pulled me out the door…

"Beautiee – slow down!" I laughed…

"Sorry – I'm just excited – I can't wait to see you in your wedding dress…" she said as we got in the car and drove off…

"Bazil…"

"Yes Chandler?"

"I hope we end up like you and Beautiee…"

"As long as you're a better man than I am… you'll be fine…"

"You're a good man Bazil…"

"Am I?"

"What's with you?"

"Nothing..."

"Well – we might as well go shopping too..."

"You're not serious..."

"Hell yea I'm serious!"

"Shopping? Really Chandler?"

"Look – we go to the tuxedo spot – we get fitted – and then we go to Bar Louie for a couple of hours..."

"Now that's more like it!" Bazil laughed... "You had me worried for a minute..."

"You're going to be my father-in-law..."

"I know..."

"You don't understand..."

"Okay..."

"You gave me your blessing – me – of all people..."

"What do you mean?"

"I'm the Sergeant at the precinct where Detective Jones arrested you – and your wife – and you still gave me your blessing – you gave me your daughter – you could've told me hell no..."

"Would you have listened?"

"Probably not..."

"So what difference does it make then?"

"I'm my father's son..."

"Okay..."

"I know I could marry Starr with or without you blessing – but I have your blessing – you see me – Chandler – you don't see the

Sergeant – you see the man that loves your daughter – that means everything to me..."

"I see the man my daughter sees – and that's why you have my blessing – but the main reason you have my blessing..."

"What? What were you gonna say?"

"The main reason you have my blessing... is because you respected me enough to ask me for it..."

"Hi Mommy! I said when she got in the car...

"Hi Starr – good morning Beautiee – where are we going?"

"Good morning Mary – we're going to David's Bridal in Orange..."

"Oh wow – I've never been there..."

"Me either Mommy – did you go to David's Bridal Beautiee?"

"Yes Starr..." Beautiee answered as she drove...

"You went to David's Bridal in Orange?" my mother asked...

"I went to David's Bridal in Vegas..." Beautiee answered. I could tell she was pre-occupied but I didn't want to push it by asking her about it...

"Damn – I could sure use a cup of coffee..." my mother said...

"When we get to David's Bridal, there's a Subway across the street and a gas station – we can stop in there for coffee if you want..." Beautiee said...

"Thank you Beautiee – I just ain't right without my coffee..."

"I know what you mean – thank God Baby Osgood lets me keep it down..."

"You get morning sickness?"

"Not really – but Mary – I need to ask you something..."

"Okay – what?"

"Was Starr born premature?"

"Yea – how'd you know?"

"I have a feeling Baby Osgood will be here before my due date..."

"Just like Bazil..." my mother laughed...

"What's that supposed to mean?" Beautiee asked...

"Oh – I just mean he's not waiting – he wants out now – Starr was the same way..."

"Oh..."

"Mommy – you never told me I was premature..."

"Yes honey – you were about a month early – I tried to keep you in the oven for 9 months but at 8 months – you were done!" my mother laughed...

"How many months are you Beautiee?" I asked...

"I'll be 8 months on your wedding day..."

"Oh wow!" I laughed...

"How've you been feeling Beauiee?" my mother asked...

"To be honest – I'm tired Mary..." Beautiee sighed. I had a feeling Beautiee wanted to say more. She had this look on her face that made me think she could explode at any moment...

"I know the feeling..." my mother said... "I was always tired when I was pregnant with Starr...

"How was your labor Mary?" Beautiee asked...

"It was hard – my water broke and those pains came hard and fast..."

"Oh so no 18-24 hour labor?"

"Hell no – thank God – I don't think I could've tolerated 18-24 hours of that!"

"How many hours were you in labor?'

"I was in labor 10 hours..."

"Oh my God – Mommy – I'm sorry!"

"You don't need to apologize honey – that's how it is with your first..."

"Chandler will be there when I have children – he'll help me with the labor..."

"Yes he will – and sex will help too..."

"Mommy!"

"I'm just tellin' you like it is!" my mother laughed. I saw Beautiee was laughing too and it made me feel a little better.

"Mommy – look! We're here! I'm so excited!"

"Le'me park the car Starr..." Beautiee laughed...

"Can I still get my coffee?"

"We can go if you want Mary – but I don't know if they'll let you inside with it..."

"Never mind..." my mother sighed...

"C'mon Mary – you can get a small cup to get you through this..." Beautiee laughed as we all crossed the street and went into the gas station..."

"Why are we here? Didn't you say we could go to Subway?" my mother asked...

"The coffee is always better at gas stations..." Beautiee answered...

"Okay – I'll be quick..." my mother said as she made her coffee..."

"Let me pay for this and we can be on our way..." my mother said...

"I already took care of it..." Beautiee said...

"Thank you..."

"You're welcome – c'mon – Starr's getting ansy..." Beautiee said as I ran across the street and beat them to the entrance...

"Beautiee?" Mary whispered...

"Yes Mary?"

"Are they expensive?"

"It depends on what you want..."

"I don't have anything nice to wear to the wedding..."

"Don't worry about it Mary – let's just get inside..."

"Beautiee?"

"Yes Mary?'

"I need to talk to you... about Bazil..."

"Do me a favor – don't open your fuckin' mouth about my husband – okay?"

"Fine! Starr – wait a minute..." my mother said as she ran up to me..."

"Everything okay?" I asked as Beautiee caught up to us...

"Everything's fine – your mother and I were discussing dresses..." I knew there was more to it but I really wanted to get inside so I didn't say anything...

"Welcome to David's Bridal – may I help you?"

"She's getting married on Thursday, June 6th..." Beautiee answered...

"Will you be needing dresses as well?"

"Yes we will..." Beautiee answered...

"Which one of you is the Mother of the Bride?"

"I am..." my mother beamed..."

"Will you be wearing a white dress?"

"Yes she will!" Beautiee answered before we could say anything...

"About what size are you?"

"I'm a size 8..."

"Dresses in your size are in the back to the right – dressed for you ladies are to the left – my name is Lisa – take your time – when you're ready I'll come assist you..."

"Thank you Lisa..." Beautiee said as she took my hand and took Mommy by the arm... "Let's go ladies – somebody's getting married!" Beautiee said as she smiled...

"Oh my God – there's too many dresses..." I laughed...

"I'll help you – did you look at the website?" Beautiee asked...

"Yes – but there's so many!"

"Okay – we know you want a white dress – right?"

"Yes!"

"Okay – do you want a dress that comes out like Cinderella or do you want a dress that shows your curves?"

"I wanna show off my curves..."

"Okay – they have a Mermaid Trumpet and they have Sheath – the Mermaid comes out at the bottom and the Sheath goes straight down – I think you should go with the Mermaid because it will accentuate your curves – I'll show you – this is a Mermaid Trumpet style – this is a Sheath style – which one do you like?"

"Mommy – help me... please..."

"Take one of each – try them both on – see which one you like the best..." my mother said...

"That's a good idea Mommy – thank you..." I said as I started looking at the dresses... "I like this one!" I yelled as I picked up the Sweetheart Trumpet Wedding Dress with Beads Sash...

"It's beautiful..." Beautiee said...

"It is beautiful..." my mother said...

"Go try it on Starr..." Beautiee said...

"Okay – I'll be right back..."

"Mary?"

"Yes Beautiee?"

"She's going to need some help..." Beautiee laughed...

"You're right – we'll be back..." my mother laughed as we went into the dressing room. Beautiee waited outside for a few moments and I came out wearing the wedding dress and stood in front of the mirror... and I started crying...

"What's wrong Baby? You don't like it?"

"Oh my God... this is my dress..."

"Yes it is..." Beautiee said...

"Can I get it?"

"Of course..." Beautiee said...

"Chandler's going to fall in love with you all over again..." my mother said...

"Yes Mary – he sure is... C'mon – let's get this dress off..." Beautiee said as Lisa came over...

"How's it going?"

"She found her dress..." my mother said...

"Wonderful! Do you want the veil, the necklace, and the pearl bracelets as well?"

"Can I get them Beautiee... please?"

"Of course..."

"Oh Beautiee – thank you, thank you, thank you!" I yelled as I jumped up and down hugging her...

"You're welcome..." Beautiee laughed...

"What size shoes do you wear?" Lisa asked...

"I wear a size 6..."

"Okay then – you'll need three pairs of shoes..."

"Why do I need three pair of shoes?"

"You need one to wear while you're getting ready, one for the ceremony, and one for the reception..."

"I'll just take two pair – I don't need shoes to wear while I'm getting ready..."

"Okay – here's our catalog of wedding shoes – personally I think you should go with the High-Heeled Sandals with Crystal Flower Strap by Vera Wang – they'll bring out the crystal in your dress and show off your pedicure..."

"I love them!"

"Yes Starr – you can have them..." Beautiee laughed...

"Okay – now you'll definitely want to be comfortable at the reception – here's our catalog of wedges and flats..."

"I want these!" I yelled as I pointed at the Crystal-Topped Wedge Sandals with Ankle Strap...

"Nice choice!" I'll put everything up front with your name on it – what's your name?"

"Starr – S-T-A-R-R…"

"Okay Starr…" Lisa said as she took everything up front…

"Are you getting a maternity dress Beautiee?" my mother asked…

"No – they're too plain – I'll just get a plus size – they have a better collection…" Beautiee said as she started looking at dresses… "Found it!" Beautiee said as she pulled a Blush Satis Plus Size Ball Gown with Crystal Pockets off the rack…

"Oh wow – try that on – le'me see!" my mother said…"

"Okay – I'll be right back…"

"You need any help?"

"Sure Mary – thanks…" Beautiee said as they went into the dressing room together. I waited until they came out and Beautiee went in front of the mirror…

"Beautiee! You look pretty!"

"Thank you Starr…"

"It looks good on you Beautiee…" my mother said…

"Thank you – I'm taking it…" Beautiee said…

"Oh my God – the dresses for the Mother of the Bride are gorgeous – how will I ever choose?" my mother asked…

"Starr – come help me outta this dress while your mother looks at the dresses…"

Beautiee said as we went into the dressing room...

"Everything okay in there ladies?" Lisa asked...

"Yes – we'll be right out..." I said as we came out...

"I love this dress – you'll be really comfortable – how far along are you?" Lisa asked...

"I'm just about 8 months..." she answered as my mother came over with the Mauve Lace Mermaid Dress with Beaded Chiffon Capelot dress she wanted to try on...

"Oh wow – that's nice!" Beautiee said...

"This is the last one we have in this color – it's a size 10 – do you think it'll fit?" Lisa asked...

"Of course – I'm not the one who's pregnant..." my mother laughed...

"Shut the fuck up!" Beautiee laughed...

"Don't hate..." my mother laughed...

"C'mon Mommy –let's try it on!" I yelled as I pulled her towards the dressing room...

"Thank God – I can sit for a few..." Beautiee said as she sat down...

"Are you okay?" Lisa asked...

"Yea – I just can't be on my feet too long..." Beautiee breathed...

"Oh wow – you look great in that dress!" Lisa yelled when we came out the dressing room. My mother looked in the mirror, and then she turned around and stuck her tongue out at Beautiee...

"That's okay – I'ma have this baby soon – then we'll see who looks better in a dress..." Beautiee laughed...

"Okay Ladies – I know you want comfortable shoes..." Lisa laughed as she showed Beautiee the catalog...

"I want these right here..." she said as she pointed to the Pink Paradox Strappy Shimmer T-Strap Mules...

"What size?"

"Size 8..."

"Okay – how about you?" Lisa asked as she showed the catalog to my mother...

"I'll take these right here..." my mother said as she pointed to the Wendie Glitter Peep Toe Wedge...

"And what size do you need?"

"Size 6 – 'cause – unlike somebody else – my feet ain't swollen 'cause I'm pregnant..." my mother laughed...

"I'ma remember that shit next time you want a cup of coffee..." Beautiee laughed...

"Okay Ladies... now that you've picked out your dresses and your accessories – it's time to let the bride prepare for her wedding night..." Lisa said as we walked to the front of the store...

"Oh wow – I can't wait!" I yelled...

"Here's a sample of everything we have in the glass cases – take your time – if you see something you like – let me know and I'll go get it..." Lisa said as she walked away to help another customer...

"I need something for your wedding night too..." my mother laughed...

"Why Mommy – it's not your night..."

"I'm still a woman – I can look sexy – it might be just for me – but I can still look sexy – tell her Beautiee..."

"She already know – she saw me with her father up-close and personal..." Beautiee laughed...

"I'm sorry..." I said...

"Girl please – you ain't stop nothin' – did she Beautiee?" my mother asked...

"Sure didn't!" Beautiee laughed...

"I like almost everything in here..." I said as I looked through the cases...

"Take your time – pick what you want – we have all afternoon..." Beautiee said...

"Okay – I want the Silky embroidered Bride Pajama Set..."

"That's it?" Beautiee asked...

"I like those!"

"I like them too Starr – but they aren't sexy enough for your wedding night..."

"Chandler won't care – he..."

"Girl move!" my mother said as she came over to look at the cases...

"Starr – this is your wedding night – do you remember how you felt the first time you made love?"

"Yes…" I whispered as I started to cry…

"What's wrong Baby?" my mother asked as she pulled me into a hug…

"Nothing… it's just…"

"What is it Starr?" Beautiee asked…

"It was beautiful…"

"Now – I want you to take what you're feeling right now… remember how romantic it was… remember how he made you feel… and go pick out some more things…" Beautiee said…

"Okay…" I sniffed as I kept looking… 'I want this Embroidered Bride White Jean Jacket – in case it gets chilly when we're on our cruise…"

"Oh that's cute!" my mother said…

"Oh – Starr – get this!" Beautiee said as she pointed to a sleep shirt that said: I Woke Up Like This #Married…

"Okay!" I squealed…

"Mary – help me out – pick something…"

"Okay – Starr – how about the DB Exclusive Double Rhinestone Bride Satin Robe…" my mother said…

"Okay Mommy – I like that too…"

"Starr – you need this Wedding Dress Bag…" Beautiee said…

"Okay…"

"Beautiee – can I get this right here?" my mother asked as she pointed to a Blank Satin Night Shirt..."

"Sure Mary..."

"Ooohhh! I like this Bikini!" I squealed as I pointed to the Personalized Glitter Print Mrs. Bikini...

"Starr... no..."

"I can't have it?"

"You can have it – if you want it – but you shouldn't wear that on your honeymoon..." Beautiee said...

"Why not?"

"Because it draws attention between your legs – the only man that should see what's between your legs is your husband..."

"Beautiee's right..." my mother said...

"I know – I can wear it when we're out on the private balcony – or when we're out on our terrace at home!"

"Okay – that's fine – get one in every color so you have one for every day..." Beautiee said...

"I'll get red, fuchsia, turquoise, white, and black...'"

"Chandler will love it..."

"Oh he'll love it alright!" my mother laughed...

"Mommy! Stop it!"

"Once you've bloomed you can't go back to being a little girl!" my mother laughed...

"I want this Glam Script Rhinestone Mrs. Satin Robe – I can wear it with my bikini..."

"Okay..." Beautiee said...

"Starr – get these!" my mother laughed as she pointed to the Mr. Right & Mrs. Always Right Party Sunglasses...

"Oh I like those – and the Mrs. Is always right!" Beautiee laughed..."

"Okay – I'll get them – and I want these!" I said as I pointed to the Mrs. Sequin Sleep Set...

"Okay – and get this All Over Beaded Vintage Inspired Garter – you need to wear that on your wedding day under your dress..."

"Nobody's gonna see it..." I said...

"Honey – when you have your reception – Chandler will sit you in the chair, lift up your dress, and take off the garter with his teeth..." my mother said...

"Oh my God – he will?"

"Yes Starr – it's tradition..." Beautiee Said...

"Ohhh... I want this Personalized Mrs. Rhinestone Side Tie Swimsuit – in Hot Pink..."

"Oh that's pretty!" my mother said...

"Okay Starr... do you want anything else?" Beautiee asked...

"Hmmm... I do like this Personalized Glitter Print Mrs. Satin Robe..."

"Ooohhh – I like it too – and it comes in 1X/2X – that's perfect for me too..." Beautiee said...

"Ooohhh... okay – I already have one in white and black – I'll pick different colors..."

"Okay Starr..." Beautiee said. My other was quiet as she watched us...

"Okay – I'll get one for you – one for me... in red – you get one in wine – we'll both get one in fuchsia - I'll get one in coral, yellow – we'll both get one in champagne – I'll get one in black, and chocolate..." Beautiee said...

"You're not getting a night gown?"

"No Starr – they don't fit me right now anyway – and since your lil' brother's planning an early arrival – I won't need to worry about it much longer..." Beautiee laughed...

"How's everything going?" Lisa asked as she came over...

"Everything fine – we're ready..." I said as I handed her a list...

"Okay – thanks for writing this list for me – I see you have robes in snall/medium and some in 1X/2X – how would you like those personalized?"

"We'd like the bikinis and the snall/medium personalized with Mrs. Corbett – C-O-R-B-E-T-T..." I answered...

"And how would you like the rest?" Lisa asked...

"Mrs. Osgood – Capital L, small e, Capital B, small l, small a, small n, small c..." Beautiee answered...

"You're Mrs. Osgood?" Lisa asked...

"Yes I am – this is our daughter, Starr – and this is her mother, Mary..." Beautiee answered as she introduced us...

"Oh wow – I can't believe it – I'm so happy to meet all of you..." she said as she hugged us..."

"Aww... it's nice meeting you too..." I said...

"Your father was in here the other day..."

"He was?"

"Yes... he already has an account with us..."

"Oh yea – that was opened in Vegas when we were married..." Beautiee said...

"I have to say – I think it's beautiful that you're all coming together to celebrate your daughter...

"So do I..." my mother said... "Thank you Beautiee... I really appreciate it..." my mother said as she started crying...

"Don't cry Mommy..." I said as I went to hug her...

"I'm sorry... please forgive me Beautiee..."

"Beautiee? What's Mommy talking about..."

"Starr... I..."

"She's sorry she didn't want to sign the lease – but you changed your mind – you signed it – so we're good now..." Beautiee answered...

"Yea Mommy – so stop crying... okay?"

"Okay Starr..." my mother said as she wiped her eyes...

"I'll get everything ready – Beautiee – go get your car and bring it to the front – I want to get everything in the car before the guys get here..."

"The guys?" I asked...

"Yes –your father is on his way – and we can't let your fiancée see anything before your wedding..."

"Oh wow – that's great – everyone can get taken care of here – I didn't know you could take care of the guys – I thought David's Bridal was just for Ladies!" I laughed...

"So that's why Bazil kept asking me where we were going!" Beautiee laughed...

"Yes – now go get your car – and I'll make sure everything's personalized correctly..." Lisa said as she hurried off...

"Starr – you can drive right?" Beautiee asked...

"Yes..."

"Good – I need a minute to sit down – can you go get the car for me?" she asked as she handed me the keys...

"Sure!" I squealed as I took the keys and ran to get the car...

"Thank you for covering for me – I'm so sorry – I don't know what I was thinking..." Mary said...

"Mary – If you're really sorry – don't tell me you're sorry – fix it!" Beautiee snapped...

"I will – I'll fix it – I promise..."

"I'll believe it when I see it..."

"Please don't tell Starr..."

"I haven't said anything yet have I?"

"No... you haven't..."

"Alright then..."

"Here's your keys – thanks for letting me drive your car..." I said...

"Thank you for calling David's Bridal – this is Lisa... Yes Mr. Osgood – we'll see you soon..." Lisa said as she hung up...

"C'mon –let's get outta here!" Beautiee said as Lisa loaded everything into the car and we drove back towards Bridgeport. When we got to Bridgeport, Beautiee drove straight to my place...

"I'm kinda hungry – can we stop and get something to eat?" my mother asked...

"I'm really tired..." Beautiee answered...

"Okay – I'll get something inside..." my mother said as she got out the car..."

"Mommy – wait!" I said as I jumped out the car and ran to give her a hug..."

"I love you Starr..."

"I love you too Mommy – I'll see you Monday..."

"Monday? You're not coming by tomorrow?"

"No Mommy – I'm spending Sunday with Chandler..."

"Okay – see you Monday then..." my mother said as she went inside and closed the door...

"Thank you for calling the Cox Law Firm – this is Dominique – how may I help you?"

"Hello Dominique – this is Mary Smith..."

"Hello Ms. Smith – the papers were served on Thursday..."

"I know... that's what I'm calling about..."

"Is there a problem?"

"Yes..."

"Hold on – le'me get Mr. Cox for you..." Dominique said as she put Mary on hold... "Mr. Cox?"

"Yes Dominique?"

"I have Mary Smith on the phone..."

"Okay – put her through..."

"Okay..." Dominique said as she put Mary through to Conrad...

"Hello Mary – the papers were served on Thursday..."

"I know... that's why I'm calling..."

"What's wrong Mary?"

"I want to withdraw my lawsuit..."

"Mary?"

"Yes Mr. Cox?"

"Did Bazil threaten you?"

"No..."

"Then why?"

"I just had a change of heart..."

"What happened between the time you spoke to me and today?"

"My daughter's getting married on June 6th..."

"So?"

"So... I'm invited... and they're paying for everything – including me..."

"Le'me get this straight – you're trading a lawsuit of $150,000 – for a dress, some shoes, and some got damned cake?"

"Mr. Cox – you don't understand..."

"Mary – it's fine – come see me on Monday morning – be here no later than 10 a.m."

"Okay Mr. Cox – thank you for understanding..." she said as Conrad hung up on her...

"Shit! Fuckin' Bitch! Dammit!" Conrad said as he threw everything on his desk onto the floor...

"Oh my God – Mr. Cox – what happened?"

"She wants to withdraw the lawsuit!"

"Okay – I'll start the paperwork..."

"Don't start anything yet –matter-of-fact – go home..."

"Did I do something?"

"No Dominique – it's Saturday – go spend some quality time with Sheldon – I'll pay you for the day – see you Monday..." Conrad said as he smiled...

"Thank you Mr. Cox! I'ma call my husband right now..." she said as she started dialing... "Babe – guess what?" Dominique said as her husband answered...

"What Babe?"

"Mr. Cox said I can leave early –he told me go spend some quality time with my husband!"

"Why?"

"Who cares – hurry up before he changed his mind!" she laughed...

"Alright – I'll be there in a few..." Sheldon said as he hung up, got in the car, and headed to the law office. When Sheldon got there, Conrad came out to greet him...

"Hello Sheldon – nice to see you..."

"Hello Mr. Cox – nice to see you too – thank you for letting my wife spend some quality time with me..."

"You're welcome – now go on – get outta here..."

"Okay then – bye!" Dominique laughed as they left. Conrad got up, locked the door, went back into his office, and made the call...

"Hey Conrad..."

"Did you get the information I sent you?"

"Yea – you sure about this?"

"Hell yea –that Triflin' Bitch just cost me $50,000 – she gonna run me my money... or she's gonna die..."

"I love you Beautiee..."

"I love you too Starr..."

"You're upset with my mother..."

"Yes Starr…"

"Thank you for not lying to me…"

"You're welcome…"

"You still kept your promise…"

"I did…"

"Why?"

"Starr?"

"Yes Beautiee?"

"I'm tired…"

"I know…"

"We're here…"

"I can't wait – can you help me get my things out the car?" I asked as I jumped out…

"No…"

"Okay… sigh… I'll do it myself…" I said as I started to go in the trunk…

"Starr!"

"Yes?"

"You can't take your things…"

"Why?"

"Because Chandler can't see anything until your wedding night…"

"Oooohhh…"

"It's tradition…"

"Ooohhh – I thought you were mad at me…"

"I'm not mad at you Starr…"

"But you're mad at my mother…"

"Starr – I'm about to get mad…"

"Okay okay – I'm sorry – I won't bring it up again – I promise…"

"Thank you!" Beautiee breathed. She got out the car and I could see she was really tired... "Give me a hug..."

"Okay..." I said. I hugged Beautiee and I felt something... "Beautiee?"

"Yes Starr?"

"Are you going straight home?"

"Yes Starr..."

"Good..."

"I'll see you soon..."

"Beautiee?"

"Yes Starr?"

"When do I get my things?"

"On your wedding day..."

"I have to wait a whole week?"

"Yes Starr – on your wedding day – we have to keep the tradition – you'll get dressed at the Bed & Breakfast – and your things will be in your room..."

"Okay... sigh..."

"I'll see you soon Starr... and you'll be Mrs. Corbett..."

"Yea..."

"Bye..."

"Bye..." I said as Beautiee drove off. As soon as I got inside, I called my father...

"Daddy?"

"Yes Starr?" my father answered...

"I'm worried about Beautiee..."

"That's sweet Starr..."

"Daddy – listen!"

"Okay..."
"Daddy – I gave Beautiee a hug..."
"That's nice..."
"Daddy – I felt something..."
"You did?"
"Daddy – please stay close to her..."
"Okay Starr – I will – I promose..."

"Oh thank God I'm home!" Beautiee said as she parked the car... "I can't wait to get all this into the house – I'm tired..." she said as she opened the trunk and took the bags, a few at a time, to the door. When she was done with the bags, she picked up the dress, put it over her arm, went to the door, unlocked it, put all the bags inside, and locked the door... "Ima get these bags upstairs, get myself something to eat, and go to bed..." she said as she brought all the bags upstairs and put them all in the guest room. "Now I can get myself something to eat..." she said as she went back downstairs to the kitchen... "Oh good – plenty of food left from the other day – I'm starving!" she said as she made herself a healthy bologna, ham, roast beef, turkey, and Swiss cheese sandwich... "Damn this shit is good!" she said as she finished her sandwich and poured some sparkling cider... "Soon this is going to be champagne..." she said as she drank until she was full... "Time to go upstairs..." she yawned as she went upstairs to the guest room, went inside, locked the door, got in the bed, and went to sleep.

Chapter 16

"They gone?" Troy asked as he came inside...

"They're gone..." Bazil answered...

"How much time we got?"

"Hmmm... Let's see... my wife, my daughter, her mother... and a black American Express card..."

"Shit – we good for the rest of the day!" Troy said as they both laughed...

"Bazil – we good?" Smalls asked as he came in...

"We good c'mon in – we're in the living room!" Bazil answered...

"Hey Troy..." Smalls said when he saw him...

"Hey Smalls..." Troy said...

"Who we waiting for?" Smalls asked...

"Chandler... and Charles..." Bazil answered...

"Who's Charles?" Smalls asked...

"His neighbor..."

"Cool..." Troy said...

"Where's everybody at?" Chandler asked as he came in with Charles...

"We're in the living room!" Bazil yelled...

"Hey!" Chandler said as he came into the living room...

"Hey Chandler..." Bazil said as he got up and gave Chandler a hug...

"Hey Dad..."

"You must be Charles – I'm Bazil..." he said as he shook Charles hand...

"Wow – Bazil Osgood – in person..."

"You've heard of me?"

"Hell yea!" Charles exclaimed...

"I'm Chandler..." Chandler said as he shook Charles hand and everyone laughed...

"I'm Troy..." Troy said as he shook Charles hand...

"I'm Smalls..." Smalls said as he shook Charles hand...

"So... y'all brothers?"

"Yea..." Bazil answered before Troy or Smalls could answer...

"Who's driving?" Chandler asked...

"Nobody..." Bazil answered...

"Nobody?" Charles asked...

"We're drinking..." Bazil answered...

"Oh... okay!" Charles laughed...

"Speaking of drinking – where we goin'?" Chandler asked...

"You'll find out when we get there – but first – we need to get there – I ordered a car for us – he should be outside now..." Bazil said as he went to the door... "It's here – let's go..." Bazil said as he opened the door and they all went outside and got in the limousine. Bazil smiled to himself watching the way Charles was in awe...

"Where we goin' first?" Charles asked...

"We're going to David's Bridal..." Bazil answered...

"Isn't that for Women?"

"It's for Men too..." Bazil answered...

"Hmmm... okay... I need some coffee..." Charles said...

"I need some Henney!" Chandler said as everyone laughed...

"We need to drink coffee before we drink anything else..." Bazil said... "Unless you don't drink coffee – then you need milk – but we're all men here – right?"

"Right!" they answered in unison....

"Okay – Mike – pull into the Dunkin Donuts on the left..."

"Yes Mr. Osgood..." Mike answered as he pulled into the parking lot... "Would you like to go through the drive through or shall I park?"

"Let's go through the drive through..."

"Yes Mr. Osgood..." Mike said as he drove the limousine around to the drive through..."

"Oh my God – look!" Margaret said as she looked out the window...

"I wonder who it is?" Nicky asked as she followed her mother to the window...

"Me too – hurry up – and make sure you don't mess up their order..." Margaret said...

"Welcome to Dunkin Donuts – may I take your order?"

"Yes Maam – hold on one moment – Mr. Osgood - what would you like?" Mike asked...

"Excuse me – did you say Mr. Osgood?" Margaret asked excitedly...

"Yes Maam..."

"Oh my God – Nicky – it's Mr. Osgood!"

"Where?" Nicky asked...

"In the limousine!"

"Oh my God – Mr. Osgood is in the limousine? Outside? Le'me see!" Anshise exclaimed as she came running to the window...

"You can't see him – he has tinted windows..." Margaret laughed...

"Ask him to put the window down – I wanna say hello!" Anshise exclaimed...

"Mr. Osgood?" Margaret asked...

"This is Mike – we'll be ready to order in a minute..."

"My employees want to know if you can put the windows down so they can say hello..."

"Mr. Osgood – the ladies wanna say hello – is it okay if I put the windows down?"

"Sure Mike – go ahead..." Bazil answered...

"Hi Mr. Osgood – I'm Margaret, this is my daughter Nicky, and this is Anshise..."

"Hello ladies – it's nice to meet you..." Horns could be heard throughout the parking lot as people became annoyed... "Sorry we're holding up the line ladies..."

"They have two choices – they can wait – or they can leave – how can we help you Mr. Osgood?"

"We'll have six medium coffees – hazelnut swirl – with cream..."

"Coming right up Mr. Osgood – Nicky – Anshise – six medium coffees – hazelnut swirl – with cream – please drive up to the pick-up window..." Margaret said and then she took the next person...

"Who the hell was that – the president?" the customer snapped...

"Maybe..." Margaret said as Anshise came to the window with the coffees...

"Here you are..." Anshise said as she passed the coffees to Mike...

"Thank ya Maam..." Mike said as he took the coffees and passed them back to Bazil, Chandler, Troy, Smalls, and Charles... "Here's the credit card..." Mike said...

"Oh that won't be necessary – my manager took care of it..." Anshise said...

"Okay – thank ya Maam... have a good day..." Mike said as he closed up the windows and drove off... "Thanks for the coffee Mr. Osgood..."

"You're welcome Mike..."

"Thank you Mr. Osgood..." Charles said...

"Please – call me Bazil..."

"Okay... thank you Bazil..."

"You're welcome..."

"You must get this a lot..." Charles said...

"I do..."

"My wife loves your authors..."

"Thank you..."

"She's always buying books..."

"Has she bought any of my wife's books?"

"Your wife writes too?"

"Yes..."

"Oh wow – I'll let my wife know..."

"My wife's always giving out review copies – I can get you an autographed copy..."

"Thank you!" Charles exclaimed as they all finished their coffee..."

"Mr. Osgood – we're here – would you like for me to wait in the parking lot for you?"

"Yes Mike..." Bazil answered...

"Okay – do you mind if I park, go get some breakfast – and come right back?"

"That's fine Mike..."

"Okay – thank you Mr. Osgood – I'll let you out..." he said as he got out and opened the door for them..."

"You ready Chandler?" Bazil asked...

"Yea... I think..."

"Don't be nervous – it's just the first day of the rest of your life..." Charles said...

"Exactly – pop ups at the job – angry texts when you don't respond in two seconds – mood swings..." Troy laughed...

"Yo – wait – the best is when she expects you to know why she mad talkin' 'bout you know what the fuck you did!" Smalls laughed...

"Oh my God – yes!" Troy said as they all laughed...

"Ummm... y'all are not helping..." Chandler laughed as they all went inside...

"Welcome to David's Bridal – my name is Lisa – I'll be taking care of you this afternoon – may I have your name please?"

"Bazil Osgood..."

"Mr. Osgood – welcome back – it'll be my pleasure to take care of your wedding needs – who's the lucky groom?"

"My future son-in-law – Chandler Corbett..." Bazil answered as he brought Chandler up to the front...

"Oh my – I'm going to love this..." Lisa said as she ran her hands down Chandler's shoulders and across his chest...

"T'ma need you to slow down Lisa...." Chandler said...

"Oh my goodness – I'm sorry – I didn't mean to offend you – I was just taking a quick measurement – everyone else uses measuring tape but I'm usually pretty accurate by feeling my way around..." she laughed...

"Shit – you ever have any wives run up on you when you're feeling on their husbands?" Smalls asked...

"A few – but I don't take it personal..."

"So... you need to feel your way around me?" Charles laughed...

"Yes... if you're buying a suit..."

"Hmmm... okay..."

"C'mon guys — let's get you in and out..." she said as she took them in the back to the men's section... "We have complete packages starting at $99.00..." she said as they started looking at suits... "We have Black by Vera Wang and Joseph Abound — personally I think Joseph Abound is the right choice for you..."

"Why?" Chandler asked...

"Black men are built different — you have broad chests and shoulders — white men are more straight up and down with small, round butts..."

"Okay!" Troy laughed...

"When you've been feeling men as long as I have — you get to know all the shapes and sizes..." Lisa laughed...

"What colors do you have?" Smalls asked...

"We have black, gray, and navy..."

"I'd like navy..." Chandler said...

"Okay — I'll be back with the suit and the accessories — what size shoe do you wear?"

"I'm a nine..."

"Okay — I'll be right back..."

"Nice choice..." Bazil said...

"Thanks Dad..."

"Here you are..." Lisa said as she came back with everything..."

"Hmmm... a pink tie..." Chandler said...

"Try it on – it looks great with the navy – and it'll also go great with your complexion..."

"Thank you – I'll be right back..." Chandler said as he went into the dressing room...

"Oh wow..." Bazil said when Chandler came out and stood in front of the mirror...

"You look good Chandler..." Smalls said...

"That's the one..." Troy said...

"Okay Chan!" Charles said...

"You look great!" Lisa said...

"I'll take everything..." Chandler said...

"Okay – I'll bring these items up front and I'll be right back..." she said as she took the items to the front...

"So what color should we get?" Troy asked...

"I like the dark gray..." Smalls said...

"So do I..." Charles said...

"I like the dark gray too..." Troy said...

"I like the black one..." Bazil said...

"Have you all decided what you'd like?" Lisa asked...

"I'd like the Black suit..." Bazil said as he went over to Lisa...

"Mr. Osgood – I don't need to feel you up – we have your measurements from your wedding..." she laughed...

"You came to David's Bridal for your wedding?" Charles asked...

"Yes..."

"Where were you married?"

"In Vegas..."

"Oh nice! They have a David's Bridal in Vegas?"

"Yes they do..."

"Mr. Osgood – would you like all the accessories?"

"Yes Lisa..."

"How 'bout the tie?"

"I'll take it..."

"That Monaco Quartz will look great on you – I'll be right back..." she said as she went to get the suit and accessories, and then she took them up front... "I took everything up front – is that alright?"

"That's fine..."

"Okay then – who am I feeling up next?" Lisa asked as she put up her hands...

"Me..." Charles laughed as he walked over to her and she felt his shoulders, his chest, and put her arms around his waist...

"Hmmm... I got it – what size shoes?"

"I'm a nine..."

"Okay – I'll be back in a sec..." Lisa came right back and handed everything to Charles...

"Thank you Lisa..." Charles said as he sat down...

"You're welcome – aren't you going to try it on?"

"I'ma wait for them..."

"Okay – who's next?" Lisa said as she put up her hands...

"Me..." Troy said as he went over to Lisa and she felt his shoulders, his chest, and hugged him...

"Ummm... okay..." Troy laughed...

"I'm sorry – you're not as tall as Chandler..." she laughed...

"Oh – so you hug the short men..." Troy laughed...

"Yes – if they let me – hugging them gives me a more accurate measurement..."

"Okay – last but not least – come here..." she said as she went over to Smalls, felt his shoulders, his chest, and hugged him... "Hmmm... - you're both just about the same – If I didn't know any better I'd say you were brothers..." she said as she went to the back..."

"She's good..." Charles laughed...

"I wonder if she's married..." Troy said...

"I sure wouldn't want my wife feeling on men all day..." Smalls said...

"Wouldn't bother me one bit..." Bazil said...

"Yea right!" Troy laughed...

"I'm serious..." Bazil said...

"Seriously?" Charles asked...

"Charles..." Bazil said as he went over to Charles and put his arm around him... "The only dick my wife wants... is mine..."

"I know that's right!" Chandler said as they high-fived...

"Okay guys – here ya go..." Lisa said as she handed Troy and Smalls the suits and accessories...

"Thank you Lisa..." they said in unison...

"You're welcome – now go try those on – I wanna see!"

"Okay, okay..." Charles laughed as they went to try on everything...

"You're a lucky man Mr. Osgood..."

"And a blessed man..." Bazil said...

"Amen – I can't wait to meet my husband..."

"You're not married?"

"Not yet..."

"I like that..."

"You like that I'm not married?"

"I like that you have hope..."

"Of course I do – every time I doubt my husband is out there – men and women come in here – God is showing me that my day is coming..."

"It is..." Bazil said as he smiled at Lisa...

"Thank you Mr. Osgood..." Lisa said as she hugged Bazil...

"You're welcome..." Bazil said as Smalls, Troy, and Charles came out...

"Oh my God – I need a phone – gimmie a phone..."

"Here – take mine..." Bazil said...

"Okay guys – he's your first picture – get in there..."

"Wait – Chandler and Bazil aren't wearing their clothes..." Charles said...

"Doesn't matter..." Lisa said as she took the picture... "Here Mr. Osgood..." she said as she handed Bazil the phone... "Okay guys – go change so I can get you outta here..." she said as Bazil waited with Lisa for them to come out... "Okay – I'll get these things up front... come with me..." she said as they followed her up front... "Okay – we have some other accessories here in the glass case – if you see anything you like, just let me know..." she said as she went to put everything in bags...

"I like this Kimono Robe..." Chandler said...

"I like it too..." Charles said...

"Get it..." Bazil said...

"Okay..." Chandler said... "But I need you to get these cuff links..." Chandler said as he pointed to the cuff links...

"Aww... that's what's up..." Troy said...

"Best Dad... nice..." Smalls said...

"Chandler... that isn't necessary..." Bazil said...

"I'ma tell you like you told me – get it..." Chandler said as they all laughed...

"Fine – I'll get it – thank you Chandler..."

"You're welcome... Dad..."

"I love y'all..." Charles said...

"Okay – everybody's getting this money clip!" Bazil exclaimed...

"Okay!" they all said in unison…

"And everybody needs to have it in their pocket on Chandler's wedding Day…"

"Okay!" they all said in unison again…

"I like these aprons for the kitchen…" Chandler said…

"Okay – let's get 'em…" Bazil said..

"How's everything going?" Lisa asked as she came over…

"I'd like the Kimono Robe…" Chandler said…

"Okay – spell your name for me…

"C H A N D L E R"

"Okay – what else?"

"The Best Dad cuff links…"

"Okay – what else?"

"Five Personalized Money Clips…" Bazil said…

"Five? Okay – give me your initials…"

"WJL…"

"Okay – who's next?"

"T.C." Troy answered…

"Next?"

"J.S." Smalls answered…

"C.C." Chandler answered…

"C.T." Charles answered…

"Okay – anything else?"

"The personalized aprons…"

"Okay – what names would you like?"

"Mrs. Corbett for the black one – Mr. Corbett for the white one…"

"Is that C O R B E T T?"

"Yes..."

"Okay – it'll be a little while to get your items customized – you guys wanna go out for a bit and come back?"

"Naa... we'll wait..." Bazil answered...

"You sure? It's gonna be about an hour..."

"Okay – we'll come back..." Bazil answered... "C'mon guys – let's get outta here for a bit..." Bazil said as he went out and they followed him to the limousine...

"Hey guys – how'd everything go?" Mike asked...

"Everything's fine Mike..." Bazil answered as they got in the limousine...

"You headed back home?"

"Not yet..."

"Where shall I take you next?"

"Andinis..."

"Okay Mr. Osgood – Andinis it is..."Mike said as they drove off towards the restaurant...

"What kind of restaurant is Andinis?" Charles asked...

"It's Italian..."

"Nice..." Charles said...

"It is – I've been there myself..." Mike said...

"Oh...."

"We're here – I'll let you out..." Mike said as he got out and opened the door for them...

"Thank you Mike – we'll see you in about an hour..." Bazil said as they went into the restaurant...

"Welcome to Andinis – nice to see you again Mr. Osgood – right this way..." the hostess said as she took them to the table... "The waitress will be here to take your orders – we have some new items on the menu..." the hostess said...

"Hello Mr. Osgood – nice to see you again..." Carmen said as she came over to the table... "May I start you off with some appetizers?"

"Yes – we'll have Risotto Balls, Veal Meatballs, Rabe & Sausage, Fried Calamari – and Samuel Adams for everybody..."

"Okay – I'll be back with your drinks and appetizers..." she said as she went to place the order...

"This is my first time here..." Charles said...

"You'll like it..." Bazil said as Carmen came back with their beers and put them on the table...

"To Chandler..." Bazil said as he raised his glass...

"To Chandler..." they all said in unison...

"I'm proud to have you as my son-in-law..."

"Thanks Dad..." Chandler said and then they all took a sip...

"Starr's a lucky woman..." Troy said...

"Starr's a lucky woman!" they all said in unison and then they all took a sip...

"Chandler's a lucky man..." Smalls said...

"I'm a lucky man!" Chandler said...

"Here! Here!" they all said in unison and then they all took a sip...

"To the brother I always wanted... but never had..." Charles said...

"Thanks Charles..." Chandler said...

"To the brother Charles always wanted... but never had!" they all said in unison and then they all finished their beers...

"Here are your appetizers..." Carmen said as she placed them on the table... "Can I get you refills?"

"Yes – please..." Bazil said...

"Coming right up..." Carmen said as she took their glasses and then went to get them refills...

"Eat! Eat!" Bazil said as everyone started eating...

"Here's your drinks..." Carmen said as she put their beers on the table... "Are you guys ready to order?"

"We'll have the NY Strip Steak..." Bazil answered...

"Regular or Cesar?"

"Regular..."

"Okay – pasta or baked potato?"

"Baked potato..."

"How would you like your steak?"

"Medium well…"

"Does that work for everybody?"

"I'd like well done…" Chandler said…

"Anyone else?"

"Well done for us too…" Smalls said…

"Yea – well done…" Troy and Charles agreed…

"Okay – medium well, 4 well-done – I'll be back…" Carmen said as she walked away…

"I can't wait for this to be over…" Chandler said…

"Over?" Bazil asked…

"I just want us to be married…"

"Aww… you love her…" Charles said…

"Yea…"

"She loves you too…" Bazil said…

"I know…"

"We were just like that in the beginning…" Charles said…

"Me 'n Keisha are still like that…" Troy said…

"My wife and I are all over each other…" Smalls said…

"Technically – Beautiee and I are still newlyweds…" Bazil said…

"Really?" Charles asked…

"We've been married a little over a year…"

"Oh wow…" Chandler said…

"We almost got divorced…" Charles said…

"What happened?" Troy asked…

"Man – we don't have enough time for that story – but we good now..." Charles answered with a smile...

"My wife asked me for a divorce..." Smalls said...

"Damn – I'm sorry..." Chandler said...

"It's okay – we good now..." Smalls said with a smile...

"I'd be devastated if Keisha ever left me..." Troy said...

"Beautiee will leave me before Keisha ever leaves you – and you already know that'll never happen..." Bazil laughed...

"You right..." Troy laughed...

"Chandler and Starr saved our marriage..." Charles said...

"Thanks – but you still wanted it to work..." Chandler said...

"Bazil and Beautiee saved my marriage..." Smalls said...

"Smalls... you never told me that..." Bazil said...

"Okay – I see how y'all get down – I'm keepin' y'all close to me so I never lose Starr..." Chandler said...

"Starr will never leave you..." Bazil said...

"I know she won't – and if she tries to leave me I'ma tell her Daddy!" Chandler said as they all laughed...

"Here's your steaks – one medium well – four well done – backed potatoes, and salads – can I get you anything else?" Carmen asked...

"Yea – A1!" Chandler answered...

"I'll be back..." Carmen said...

"Oh damn!" Charles said as he tasted his steak...

"Good – right?" Bazil asked...

"Hell yea!" Charles smacked...

"Can your wife cook steak?" Chandler asked...

"Oh yea – but this right here – she might have a lil' competition..." Charles laughed...

"Starr's like her father – she cooked for me the first night I invited her to my place ˗ I walked in from work and she had dinner ready for me..." Chandler sighed...

"Keisha gets it in – I move out her way – and stay out her way..." Troy laughed...

"Here's your A1..." Carmen said as she placed the bottle on the table... "If you need anything else – I'll be over there..." she said as she walked away and they continued...

"My wife gets down... and so do I..." Smalls said...

"I do the cooking in my house..." Bazil said...

"Your wife can't cook?" Charles asked...

"I won't let her..."

"Why?"

"I love cooking for her..."

"Aww..." Charles said...

"I can tell..." Chandler said...

"You've had his cooking?" Charles asked...

"Oh yea..." Chandler answered...

"When are we gonna taste your cooking?" Troy asked...

"Next time you're at my house and you let me know you're hungry..." Bazil laughed....

"I'm there!" Smalls said...

"Well..." Bazil said as he rubbed his stomach... "I guess we better go get our things before they think we forgot..."

"Oh my God..." Charles laughed as he got up and stretched... "I'm so full – my wife's gonna be mad if I can't eat dinner..."

"No she won't – you're with me – remember?" Chandler laughed...

"Oh yea – I'm good – she likes you..." Charles laughed as they all got up from the table...

"I'll meet you guys outside..." Bazil said as he went to pay the check...

"Thank you Mr. Osgood – always a pleasure..." Carmen said...

"You're welcome – I'll see you again..." Bazil said as he left the restaurant and went to get in the limousine...

"Back to David's Bridal?" Mike asked...

"Yes Mike..."

"Okay Mr. Osgood..." Mike said as they drove off...

"Mr. Osgood – I was just getting ready to call you…" Lisa said as they walked in…

"Is everything ready?" Bazil asked…

"Yes – let me show you how the engraved money clips came out…" she said as she took the money clips out to show them…

"Oh yes – this is exactly what I wanted…" Bazil said…

"Nice… thank's Dad…" Chandler said. Troy, Smalls, and Charles nodded in approval…

"Everything's ready for you to take to the car – if you have any problems or you need anything – you can call me directly…"

"Thank you Lisa…" Bazil said…

"You're welcome Mr. Osgood – have a great day – and congratulations Chandler…" she said as she went to help another customer…

"What a great day…" Charles said as they got in the limousine…

"Yes it was…" Chandler agreed…

"Mike – we're going home…" Bazil said…

"Okay Mr. Osgood…" Mike said as he drove off. When they got to the house, Mike opened the door, Bazil got out, and took out his bags…

"Guys – we're gonna go in the library – leave your things in the car…"

"Okay…" they said in unison as they followed Bazil into the house and into the library…

"Oh wow – this is nice!" Charles said…

"Thank you Charles..." Bazil said... "Smalls, Troy – you know what to do – I'll be right back..." Bazil said as he took his bags upstairs. Troy got five glasses and Smalls got the bottle of Hennessey and poured them all drinks... "Beautiee? Beautiee – where are you? Hmmm – maybe she's in the guest room – Beautiee are you in here?" he asked as he tried to open the door but it was locked... "Beautiee... open the door... sigh... I'll deal with this later..." Bazil said as he went back downstairs to join them in the library... "Let's do this!" Bazil said as they spent the rest of the afternoon drinking, laughing, and talking.

Twisted Starr Tree

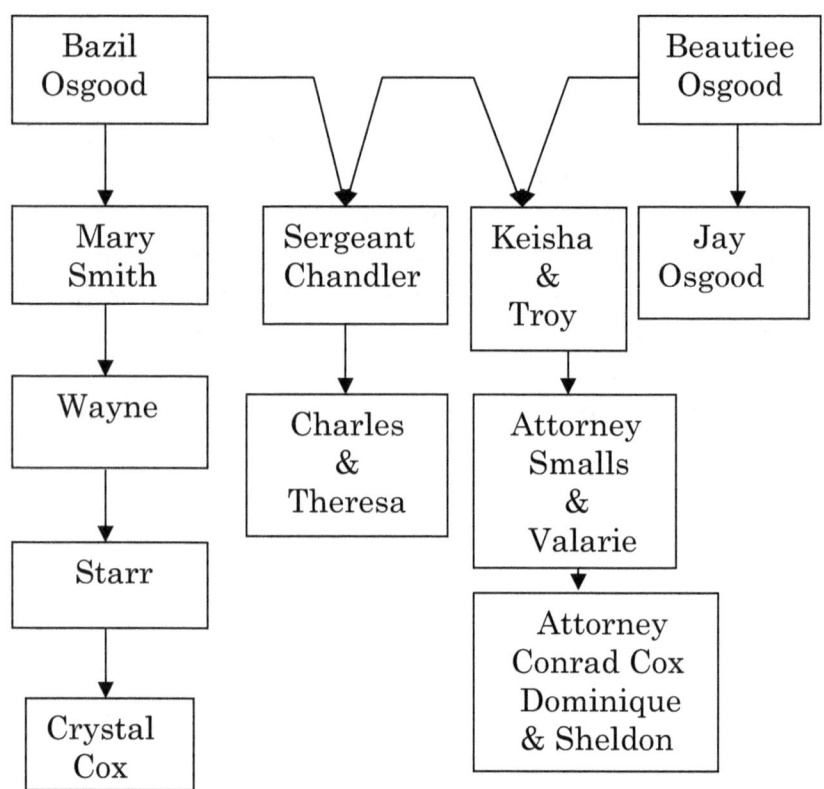

www.ingramcontent.com/pod-product-compliance
Lightning Source LLC
Chambersburg PA
CBHW072232170626
46813CB00003B/1182